MOTHER OF PEARL

Mother of Pearl

a novel

Edward Swift

British American Publishing

This novel is a work of fiction. Names, characters, places and incidents either are the product of the author's imagination or are used fictitiously. Any resemblance to actual events or locales or persons, living or dead, is entirely coincidental.

Published by British American Publishing
3 Cornell Road
Latham, NY 12110
Manufactured in the United States of America

94 93 92 91 90 5 4 3 2 1

I would like to thank the Helene Wurlitzer Foundation of New Mexico for many years of encouragement and support. I am also deeply grateful to the MacDowell Colony, the New York Foundation for the Arts, James Stein, and Margaret Mirabelli.

Library of Congress Cataloging-in-Publication Data

Swift, Edward, 1943-
    Mother of pearl : a novel / Edward Swift.
        p.   cm.
    ISBN 0-945167-26-1
    I. Title.
    PS3569.W483M68   1990
    813'.54—dc20   89-38571
                                                                        CIP

Dedicated to

Camilla Carr

ONE

The elderly McAlister sisters, Pearl in khaki pants and Wanda Gay in an organdy dress, sat on the wedding porch of their family house swinging and arguing over the placement of the new rose bushes that had arrived in the afternoon mail. The argument had begun as soon as the mailman, who always approached the McAlister residence with caution, had delivered the package, which required a signature. Both sisters had been determined to sign for it, and both had been determined to open it. With two signatures on the delivery slip—one written with the delicacy of a spider's web and the other with a heavy hand that sliced through the paper—the postman had left the sisters, each brandishing a pair of scissors, to open the package the best way they could. Together they had attacked it with scissors and clawing fingers until the string and wrapping was strewn about the porch and the rose bushes had tumbled into the yard.

"The one labeled Blood Red is mine," Wanda Gay said, going for the bush of her choice.

"You have always gone for blood, Sister." Pearl, whose hair was winter white, cradled a bush marked Pink Beauty in her arms. "I prefer softer colors myself."

Then came the argument over ownership of the third bush, as well as the proper place for planting. Wanda Gay favored the backyard, but Pearl preferred the front. The

1

argument would continue, their neighbors knew, into the afternoon and possibly the night.

As expected, Pearl, rawboned, and Wanda Gay, round and heavily powdered, carried their planting dispute through supper, the feeding of the cats, and the washing of the dishes. Famous for their perpetual spats, each sister hardly ever had a kind word for the other, yet both were easily angered by any suggestion of hatred between them.

This was their last spring together. Wanda Gay, a diabetic, was to take ill in late summer and die in the Morehope County Hospital, and Pearl, accused of her sister's death, was to last no longer than St. Valentine's Day the following year. But that early spring evening when the fireflies were swarming about their bare legs, and the candle moths were clinging to the screen door, neither sister thought of dying. Into the night they sat on the porch where their parents had been joined in wedlock and argued vociferously over placement of the Tyler roses. Their neighbors across the fence listened to every word.

"I intend to plant one of them under my window and the other two on either side of the sidewalk." Pearl held a cigarette she had just rolled herself between her tightly pursed lips and spoke around it. "I also intend to have my way, Sister. It's my green thumb not yours."

"You'll get your way over my dead body." Wanda Gay spoke in the most threatening tone her lack of energy would allow. "I will not have those rose thorns ripping my fine dresses when I decide to take the sidewalk."

"Then perhaps, Sister, you will not be taking the sidewalk any time soon," Pearl said, attempting to read the planting instructions by a shaft of light from the nearest window. "After the roses are planted you will be expected to change some of your daily habits. For example, when leaving or returning to the house you will be expected to remind yourself to use the driveway instead of the sidewalk. That won't hurt you, will it?"

"I don't see why I, a sugar diabetic invalid, should

be the one to alter my daily routine," said Wanda Gay. "That doesn't make sense to me."

"If you don't wish to ruin your dresses, it makes sense," said Pearl. Giving her total attention to the planting instructions, she abandoned the argument while Wanda Gay sulked.

Presently Wanda Gay opened a can of mixed nuts. She picked out the Brazil nuts and threw them into the street. Then she amused herself by wondering out loud what they would be doing if their brother Frank were still alive.

"Oh he's not dead," Pearl said, slowly lifting her cigarette to the center of her lips. "Not to me."

Many years earlier, while sitting on another porch in another place, she had been forewarned of her brother's death but had never been able to accept it. To Pearl, Frank was still alive and her husband Teddy was alive as well.

"Some people don't really die," she told her slightly older sister as they sipped their evening tea on the porch swing. "They go on living someplace else and not all of them in the same place either. Sometimes you have to go to a lot of trouble to find them. Sometimes you have to go to a lot of trouble to keep them alive. Sometimes there's no choice. Oh, there's so much confusion on this subject, but it's perfectly clear to me."

"Sister!" exclaimed Wanda Gay, "don't talk like that. It upsets me. Lately it has become impossible for you to answer a simple question. I asked you what you thought we'd be doing if Frank were still living and here you go talking about something that's not necessary to think about. I'm tired of your morose thoughts. You must learn to answer the questions asked of you or none at all. People ask questions for a reason, Pearl, and that reason is not very complicated: they merely want a sensible answer."

"Well what do you think we'd be doing if Brother were still alive?" asked Pearl. "Your answer is the only one you'll accept, so let's hear it."

"Thank you," said Wanda as she stirred her tea into

a whirlpool. "This is my answer: if Frank were still living today we'd be trying to get him out of jail again. How many years has it been since we made that trip to get him out of jail, Pearl?"

"I'm not going to count up the years, Sister. I don't want to know things like that. You, on the other hand, like to stir up discontent within yourself and everyone else by counting the years that have gone by, but I'm not going to give in to this insidious little game of yours."

"Well how many years has it been since Frank died, then?" Wanda Gay asked. "I count twenty-five, Sister. Is that right?"

Pearl refused to answer. She was wondering how many times her brother had been married. The number had escaped her memory. She wondered if he had loved any of his wives even half as much as she still loved Big Teddy.

From somewhere within the ruffled neckline of her dress Wanda Gay brought forth a cube of sugar and slipped it into her tea.

"I saw that," said Pearl. "You're just like Mother, always professing your illness and denying it at the same time. Sugar will eventually kill you, Wanda Gay."

"It didn't kill Mother," Pearl's diabetic sister answered.

"No, it didn't," Pearl replied. "And with Mother it probably never would have. In spite of the fact that she was always saying she was ready to die, her will to live was very strong. People who have such strong wills are determined to live and live and outlive. There's usually some meanness in them that adds to their longevity too. You, Wanda Gay, *seem* to have inherited Mother's meanness, but I have come to discover that you haven't. I know this is going to come as a shock to you, but it's the truth: you're not really mean. You're just confused. But Mother was mean, and she enjoyed being mean. Wherever she is right now she's being mean to somebody, and if I were there with her I would be saying all kinds of hateful things to her face because she always needed contention to stimulate the mean streak that kept her alive in spite of her sweet tooth."

"But what did you admire about her?" asked Wanda Gay. "Surely there was something. I, as you must know, admired Mother's beautiful hair, especially when she was young and wore it long. Now don't say you admired the same thing, Pearl. I don't want you to copy me."

"Sister, you are the last person on earth I would take as a role model," Pearl replied. "What I most admired about Mother was certainly not her hair, it was her natural, uncultivated meanness, for which she felt no remorse. She viciously protected herself and nobody else."

"Then do you think it was an accident, the way she died?" Wanda Gay asked. "I always wanted to know what you thought about that, Pearl. Was Mother's death accidental?"

"Was Frank's death accidental?" Pearl asked, preparing to roll another cigarette. "Was Daddy's? Did Perdita Fane kill herself accidentally or on purpose? Is there such a thing as an accidental death? Teddy's death. Was that an accident?"

"Oh you make everything so complicated, Pearl." Wanda Gay frowned. "If Big Teddy had lived he would have divorced you long ago. I know he would have because you didn't really love him, you just thought you did. You didn't know him long enough to love him, that's how I think. I, on the other hand, loved my husband very much, but only after I got used to him."

"After he died you suddenly decided you loved him," said Pearl. "I'll bet I know why too."

"You have always tried to make me believe that you know everything there is to be known," said Wanda Gay. "But I've come to find out that you don't know very much at all, Sister. Your complicated answers are devised to hide the truth. That's why if Big Teddy had lived he would have divorced you on account of all these complex motives and reasons and solutions you're always dreaming up. The two of you would have come to a falling-out over some very simple little problem that you would have made into the world's most complicated issue."

"I don't think so," said Pearl. When speaking of Teddy her voice became very serious. "Teddy and I had what Frank and I had, but we had something else too, we also had what Frank and I could never have."

"Sister, I hate it when you talk in riddles!" Wanda Gay shouted. "You and Frank always had a way of talking that nobody else could understand. You know how that aggravates me."

After a spell of silence, Wanda Gay spoke out again. "I sometimes wish we had another brother or sister still living don't you, Pearl? I'd like a choice of somebody else to talk to."

"Listen, Wanda Gay." Pearl flicked her ashes into the yard. "We're lucky to be here and I don't mean just on this porch swing either. Given our parents' relationship, it's a miracle that we were ever born."

"Birth is a miracle," said Wanda Gay.

"In this case I'm thinking about conception," Pearl said. "How many nights do you think Mother and Daddy slept together in the entire time they were married?"

"Pearl, I don't think that way," said Wanda Gay, slipping another cube of sugar into her tea. "I wouldn't dare."

"You should every now and then," said her sister. "It would do you some good to change your ways." Without explanation she walked inside the house while Wanda Gay pushed off in the porch swing. The chains squeaked against the ceiling hooks and the noise drifted into the yard and down the street. While Wanda swang back and forth, Pearl was in the attic searching through an old box.

"Pearl, what are you doing up there?" Wanda shouted. "I can hear you bumping around. Please don't be smoking in the attic, Sister. You know that worries me." Pearl didn't answer.

"I'm going to have to turn the porch light on now," Wanda said. "The bugs are getting too bad."

She flipped a switch and the porch was bathed in yellow light. Yellow, Wanda Gay had read, would keep the bugs away. "Pearl," she shouted. "Come back down here, I miss you when you're gone."

While she sat on the porch sipping her sweetened tea and waiting for Pearl to come back, tennis balls landed like hail stones on the front lawn. "It's tournament time again," Wanda Gay remarked. She had been saying this since the first warm day of March when the courts opened for the season. "I hate tournament time. It's my least favorite part of the year."

The tennis courts located directly behind the McAlister house had been in existence for five years, and only recently had floodlights been installed for evening games. Wanda Gay hated the courts. The noise of the balls bouncing off the roof at night threw her into fits of anger. Pearl's outrage, although somewhat calmer on the surface, was equal to that of her sister. She had already replaced three windows, doing all the work herself, and was suing the independent school system for building the courts too close to their family home.

Only Teddy III, Pearl's grandson, enjoyed having the tennis courts practically in the backyard. On his visits he would practice his serves, often with his grandmother on the other side of the net. "I hope to God Almighty no one recognizes me out here," Pearl would say. People were accustomed to seeing her in a pair of pants and a man's shirt, but when accompanying her grandson to the tennis courts she would wear a disguise: an old gingham dress and a sunbonnet. "I will lose my lawsuit if people see me out here seeming to enjoy this hideous recreation," she would remind Teddy. "In the future if anyone should ask you the identity of your attractive tennis partner, be sure to say that you do not know who I am, as my legal case against these courts is pending."

Pearl's grandson was finishing his freshman year at

the state university, where he was studying architecture, but he spent most of his time playing tennis. "Why do you have to slam the balls over the net?" Pearl asked on his recent spring break. "You know I can't retrieve them when they are that fast. You must slow down. Speed is not the most important thing in our lives. It's taken me an age to discover this."

"Why was your driver's license revoked?" Teddy asked as he served another ball. "My father wants to know."

"This is not a suitable topic of conversation for a tennis court." Pearl raised her voice. Wanda Gay could hear her all the way to the front porch. "Therefore I intend to change the subject. If your father wants the answer, let him ask. He has an educated mind, or is supposed to. Allow him to use it."

"He doesn't want me to be an architect," said Teddy.

"Allow that to be your father's problem, not your own," said Pearl. She swung at a ball and missed. "Your great grandfather was a mechanic and a carpenter as well as an architect." With her tennis racket she pointed to the McAlister house. "He built our house with his bare hands, but please don't ask me how he learned to build a house or repair a car. I cannot answer that, and neither can your learned father. Albert McAlister knew how to do a lot of things most people need to go to school to learn."

After Teddy had returned to the state university, an unavoidable loneliness crept through the McAlister house. Wanda Gay and Pearl wandered from room to room searching for something Teddy had left behind, just anything that would remind them that he had been there. What Wanda Gay hated about Teddy's visits was the emptiness she felt afterward.

"I feel like we've had another death, Sister," Wanda Gay said, while waiting impatiently for Pearl to return to the porch. "When is Teddy coming back to visit us?" She stared at the ceiling and shouted. "Are you still up there? Can you hear me? I said, When is Teddy coming back,

Sister? I don't like having to make these emotional adjustments every time he leaves."

"You should have gotten used to making adjustments a long time ago," said Pearl. Her voice drifted through the house and onto the porch. "Nobody likes to adjust their ways, but sometimes it's necessary. Tomorrow you will be forced to take the driveway instead of the sidewalk. That, for you, will be another emotional adjustment."

Wanda Gay did not catch her sister's words as they floated across the porch and into the warm evening where the crickets were competing with the swing.

"Sister, do you hear me?" asked Wanda Gay. "I said, When is Teddy coming back: I like it when he's here. I wish I had a grandchild half as smart as Teddy. All Demeris has given me is heartache and grief. You should be thankful, Pearl, that your grandson has turned out so well. Can you hear me? I said, You should be thankful your grandson has turned out to be a good boy."

"Yes, I can hear you," Pearl shouted through the floor of the attic, but again her words did not penetrate the crickets, the squeaking of the swing, or the noise of the passing cars.

"I think he's a good boy," said Wanda Gay, pouring another cup of tea and talking more to herself than her sister. "But at the same time I don't think you should have taught him how to roll cigarettes. His father is going to get mad at you for encouraging him to smoke." She raised her voice, "Sister, why does Teddy want to roll cigarettes when it's much easier to buy them already rolled up? Can you hear me?"

"Yes, I can hear you, Sister, I am not the deaf one, remember?" While searching through a box of linens, Pearl aimed her voice in the direction of the porch. "No, I am not up here smoking, so don't get nervous. I would give my left arm to have a Lucky Strike right now, but store-bought cigarettes are too expensive nowadays, especially for old people and college students. That's why I taught

9

Teddy how to roll a perfect cigarette. Daddy taught me and I thought it important to pass on this obsolete skill."

"Pearl, I can't understand a word you said," Wanda Gay shouted. "Please come down here. I want to ask you something about that trip we took that time. That trip when we tried to get Frank out of jail. That's been on my mind a lot lately. Where would we all be right now if we'd stayed at home? That's what I keep asking myself."

Moments later Pearl, dancing a feeble waltz step, returned to the porch with a sheet over her head. Wanda Gay screamed and ran into the yard. "Pearl, is that you?" she whispered. "Please explain yourself before I die of fright, you know how I am. You make me think I'm seeing a ghost."

"We all live with ghosts," said Pearl, "and they are nothing to be afraid of. What is a ghost, anyway, if not the memory of some departed soul that takes up residence inside us?" She pulled the sheet down until her nose could be seen protruding through a small hole. "You might think you're seeing a ghost, Sister, but what you're really seeing is a miracle. Your miracle. Yours, mine, and Frank's."

Pearl ran a finger through the hole and lifted the sheet off her head and body. "Through this hole, Wanda Gay, you were conceived, I was conceived, and Frank was conceived. In that order. Mother, as you surely must realize, could not stand for Daddy's flesh to brush up against hers, and to make matters worse her father threatened to disown her if she did not bring forth heirs. After Jonsey died, he relied on Mother to give him a grandson, and that's exactly what she did, whether she wanted to or not and obviously she didn't. That's also why the three of us were born within the first two and a half years of our parents' marriage. Mother wanted to get that part of her life over with as soon as possible. And after Frank was born she put the sheet away."

"You are not telling me anything I didn't already know," Wanda Gay said, her voice carrying over the fence and into the neighbor's bedrooms. "Mother always said,

'Physical intercourse is intended for procreation and not recreation.' Those were her exact words." On her swollen feet she climbed the porch steps and entered the yellow light. "I not only remember her exact words, I have them written down in a special notebook along with Mother's other clever and important sayings."

She sat down on the swing again and pushed off with disgust. "You don't know everything, Sister, you just think you do." She arranged her butterfly sleeves as she spoke. "For your information, after Frank was born Mother did not put the sheet away for good. She saved it, and when I got married she gave it to me, and I used it to conceive Demeris. Then just as soon as I found out that Demeris was on her way, I gave the sheet back to Mother because I decided that I didn't need it anymore. Now I wish I had used it just one more time."

"Oh my God," said Pearl. "I didn't know that Mother's influence had spread quite that far. Is there no escaping her, ever?"

She left Wanda Gay alone on the porch and went inside. The living room was filled with two Victorian sofas and several Queen Anne chairs, each with doilies and antimacassars. Angled into a corner a baby grand piano stood on a threadbare oriental carpet. On top of the dusty piano was a metronome which began ticking as soon as Pearl entered the room. "Not again," she said, standing before the metronome which was silent to all other ears but hers. "Allegro vivace tonight," she whispered as three of her Persian cats escaped from their upper rooms and came running down the staircase. "There was a time when Mother wanted everything played allegro vivace," she said to the cats. They followed her through the house and out the back door. So did the ticking.

The backyard was large and enclosed with a plank fence. Floodlight from the tennis courts threw long shadows across the lawn. Pearl scanned the vegetable garden, which had already been planted, but the seeds, mostly corn and peas, had not yet sprouted. Last year's scarycrow was leaning against the fence, and the day's wash was still hanging on the clothesline. She removed the wash while fireflies swarmed around her head. Then she hung her mother's sheet on the line and struck a match. "Someone should have done this a long time ago," she said while the sheet burned and the cats rubbed against her legs.

The next day she raked the ashes into the lawn.

TWO

Many years before the sheet was burned and the ashes were raked into the lawn, Frank McAlister, facing the last hour of his life, thought of his sister Pearl and that unusually hot spring ten years earlier when he had robbed a liquor store in Canton, Arkansas, and Pearl, with the entire family in her Ford, had driven all night to rescue him from what their mother had called "a shameful but totally expected disaster."

Frank died of a heart attack while watching a Carnival parade in Rio de Janeiro. He collapsed on a crowded street, and for a long time no one except a pickpocket noticed him lying there. The thief took the opportunity to examine the contents of Frank's wallet and pockets. While watching himself being robbed of a few dollars, a wristwatch, and a silver ring, Frank wondered what would have happened if he had not robbed that liquor store long ago. He wondered if this was his retribution.

On discovering a bottle of rum tucked under Frank's belt, the thief toasted his dying victim. "Safe trip, friend," he said before disappearing into the crowd.

Frank, a construction worker by profession, had been sent to Brazil to supervise the building of two bridges and a highway. Fighting to postpone his last breath, he wished that he had come to South America much earlier in his life. Again he thought of that summer when he had been sent to jail for armed robbery and his family had attempted to rescue him from an uncertain fate.

All that had happened in the spring of 1955. Frank, armed with a sawed-off shotgun he had never fired or taken the time to load, robbed the only liquor store in Canton. He made off with $68 and a bottle of whiskey but was apprehended before he reached his Plymouth parked several blocks away.

On his deathbed he recalled a single sentence that had appeared in the body of an article printed in the *Canton Star*:

This is not, the newspaper reported, *what you would call a well planned attack on a small merchant.*

Sometime later it was discovered that Frank had given the robbery a great deal of thought after all. What he had hoped to gain was a month in jail, just long enough to decide what to do about his fourth wife, Marsha. They had been living together once again, and Frank had been heard saying that he didn't feel safe with her in the house.

"If I could only find a woman like my sister Pearl," Frank had told Sam Sticks, the jailer. "I should have been looking for a woman like Pearl all my life."

"She must be a mighty special sister," Sam had said, closing the door to the jail and pretending to lock it. In his last hour Frank could still hear the hinges creaking against Sam's voice.

"I think too much of you to really lock you up, Frank. Everybody knows you didn't mean to rob Bud Johnson, even Bud himself knows it. But I've got to do what I've got to do. Everybody knows you've just had a bad year, and who wouldn't what with Marsha and all the trouble she's been causing. These days it's real easy to get yourself confused, and that's what happened. But that don't mean you'll be confused for good, with you it's just a passing thing."

In Canton, Frank had been well known and admired. "He has a *way* about him." That's what everyone said. He could walk into any room and light it up, and he always spoke to everyone by name. Sometimes he even attended the Methodist church, but more often than not, he spent his Sundays working. Like his father, he understood machinery, and could bring any kind of motor back to life again. People depended on him to repair farm equipment, or kitchen appliances, and he rarely accepted payment, other than a meal, a credit slip from a merchant, or a drink at the county line.

Frank had a mass of wavy hair and a slight hump in his predominant nose, which was usually sunburned from working out of doors. He couldn't understand why anyone would want to work inside, and that was another reason why Sam Sticks didn't lock the door to Frank's cell. "Frank hates being cooped up," Sam told his wife. "He won't be in jail very long. His company needs him too bad."

Fresh out of high school, Frank entered the army, but due to chronic attacks of asthma, he did not finish his term. On receiving a medical discharge he went to work for Brown and Brown Construction Company, the only job he had ever held. His mother, Miss Eugenia Fane McAlister (she thought Miss far more dignified than Mrs.), had always been ashamed to admit that her only son was a common laborer. "Surely he could have found a more dignified job," she often said to Pearl and Wanda Gay. "If he had only come home, I would have found him a decent and respectable way to make a living. I know all about decency and how to go out looking for it. Plus I have a respectable source of income."

Miss Fane was a piano teacher. Each year she held a recital to show off her students, and each year the same pieces were played over and over again. Her husband, Albert McAlister, had only attended two recitals in his life. "One was enough," he had said. "The second one nearly killed me. I'm a music lover at heart, that's why it was so painful." Miss Fane grew to resent what she called "Albert's crude and insensitive side," and therefore, she refused to accept his last name as her own. *Fane*, her maiden name, was the one she used to sign her checks, even before Albert had died.

Albert died before he and Pearl had had a chance to resolve their dispute over her marrying Big Teddy. He died shortly before her son was born, shortly before Big Teddy was killed in the war, and shortly after Frank had married his second wife.

"I have told Frank not to show up with that pitiful excuse for a human being," Miss Fane had told her daughters at Albert's wake. Frank was two hours late, and his mother was convinced that his lateness was intentional. "I'm telling you," she said, tapping her long, red fingernails on Albert's aluminum coffin. "Frank's out to disgrace the entire human race and get away with it. But I raised him better than that. Now one of you tell me I'm right whether you think I am or not. Even a lie will make me feel better, especially at a time like this."

"You're right, Mother," replied Wanda Gay.

"Make me sick, why don't you?" said Pearl. "There's not one thing wrong with Frank. He works very hard and always has. That's probably why he's late. He's still working."

By the time he was thirty, Frank had helped build bridges, tunnels, and highways in three states. He could drive almost any kind of equipment, but his specialty was the dragline, and his mother thought that was beneath the family's dignity.

"Operating a dragline is a decent job, Mother," Pearl argued while staring at her father's photograph displayed on the closed casket.

"It is *not* a decent job," Miss Fane replied. "That's why I tell everyone that Frank's a highway architect. I don't know if there is such a thing or not, but it sounds more dignified than running a dragline, and besides that, it's as close to the truth as I can get without telling my Sunday school class an out-and-out lie. But, of course, that's what Frank wants. He's bound and determined to make a liar of me before I die, and one of my daughters, I'm sorry to say, is right behind him."

"Pearl and Frank are just alike, Mother," Wanda Gay said, as if her sister were not present. "All they concentrate on is how to steal somebody else's thunder, how to out-shine, and out-do, and out-behave every member of this family. I hate having to say unflattering things about my only brother and sister, and tonight I will get down on my knees and ask forgiveness for this, but right now I just can't help myself: Frank and Pearl have always thought they were better than the rest of us."

"We don't think that at all," Pearl replied. "But if we are, there's nothing we can do about it, is there?"

When he drew his final breath Frank was thinking of Pearl. No one else in his family came to mind. "I wonder what she's doing," he said to a stranger who was trying to pull him away from the trampling crowd. His face was bloody. His shirt was ripped open in the front, and his shoes were missing. "I wonder where she is right now," he said as carnival floats, drifting like wingless angels, passed him by.

THREE

Frank and Pearl had always been close, but there were times when they were particularly close. The day he died, so many thousands of miles away from home, she was writing a letter to her son, a Ph.D candidate at the state university. Halfway through the letter she wrote: "Something is wrong with Frank. I don't think we will ever see him again. I told him not to go so far away." The words fell onto the paper as if someone else had written them. This was what Pearl called a *Frank feeling*, and as she watched the words forming on the page, she realized, even before the message had registered in her mind, that it was the last time she would ever know this experience.

The *Frank feeling* before this final one, which took Pearl by complete surprise, had occurred many years earlier on that hot spring day in 1955 when Miss Fane's piano students were preparing for their annual recital. That was the day Frank had robbed his friend, Bud Johnson, and almost immediately, Pearl knew that something was wrong.

She was sweeping out the Methodist church when an uncomfortable feeling of suffocation came over her. She drew deep breaths which did not satisfy her body's sudden need for oxygen. "I feel as though I'm having an asthmatic attack," she said to Lefty Simmons, the church janitor.

"You better sit down and be calm," said Lefty.

"That's what I always told Frank when he had these

smothering attacks," Pearl said. "I would put a hand on his chest and tell him to relax and in a few minutes he'd be able to breathe again. I'm not so sure I can do that for myself."

Pearl forced herself to relax on a pew while she thought of her brother, who had been discharged from the army because of chronic asthma and sleepwalking. After leaving the army he occasionally walked in his sleep but was not bothered with smothering attacks. "Frank was convinced if he came back to Morehope for any length of time he would suffocate," Pearl said. "Now I know what he was talking about."

Gradually she was able to breathe deeply again but for the rest of the morning and much of the afternoon she couldn't stop thinking about her brother. No matter what she did to distract her thoughts, Frank was foremost in her mind. "I wonder what he's up to," she kept saying. "I wonder what he's doing and if he's all right. Something tells me he's not. Something tells me we'll hear from him real soon, maybe today."

That day, Pearl, a brunette with a grey stripe running through her naturally curly hair, was decorating the sanctuary of the Methodist church where her mother's piano recital was to take place in the evening. But she was not working at her usual fast pace. "Who cares about Mother's damn piano students," she said, pressing the creases out of last year's crepe paper. "I'm having one of my *Frank feelings* today."

"I sure hope this one is better than that last one you had," said Lefty Simmons. He was rolling the pulpit to one side of the sanctuary. "And if you ever have one of your feelings about me, I sure don't want to know about it unless it's good."

This was the second *Frank feeling* Pearl had had in a little over six months. While pleating the blue paper around a crock of gladiolas, she wondered what the feeling was all about. They usually signaled bad luck and that worried her. "Maybe I'm having a good luck feeling today and I just think it's a bad luck feeling," she said. "Maybe that's it."

"Whatever you say, Miss Pearl," said Lefty Simmons. "I'm not smart enough to argue with one of your feelings. Too hot to put that kind of pressure on my kind of brain."

A little more than six months before the suffocating feeling in the church, Pearl had been taking down her Thanksgiving decorations to make way for Christmas when another *Frank feeling* had swept over her. That time she had experienced sharp pains in her legs. "I wonder what this means?" she had asked herself.

The next day she found out that Marsha had shot Frank in the leg. He had come home from work and found his wife sitting on the couch with her clothes half ripped off and scratches on her face, arms, and legs. She told Frank that a flying saucer had landed on top of their house and six Martians had forced her to enter the spacecraft on a ladder made entirely from threads of light. "You will not believe this," she said, "but the ladder dissolved into thin air once we were inside the saucer."

"Did the Martians dissolve too?" he asked.

"No, they did not," his wife answered, "they examined me from head to toe, with the most tender hands I've ever felt."

"Then how did you get all those scratches?" Frank asked.

"I clawed myself nearly to death when I realized they didn't want to take me with them," Marsha confessed.

"Did any of these Martians look like the six football players who roughed you up last week?" Frank inquired.

"Treat me with some respect," Marsha demanded.

"How can I," Frank said. "You never tell the truth. And when you do, it's so exaggerated it's not the truth anymore."

"I tell the truth all the time," Marsha said. "And I'm going to shoot you in the leg to prove it."

Frank walked into the kitchen to get a beer, and when his back was turned Marsha fired one, well-aimed shot with her daddy's pistol. When she saw blood running through Frank's pants she became hysterical. Frank couldn't tell if she was laughing or crying so he slapped her unconscious and drove her to the county jail where she confessed to Sam Sticks that men from outer space had told her to shoot her husband. While Sam locked her up, his wife helped Frank into a wheelchair and pushed him to the Canton hospital only a block away.

Three days later he was released on crutches, but by then Marsha had already been declared incompetent to stand trial. While in jail she had burned herself with cigarettes, pulled out her hair, and beaten her head against the bars—all for the love of Frank. She said she loved him so much she wanted to kill him, and on the way to the state asylum she promised herself that the next time she had an opportunity to express her feelings she'd aim a little higher.

Five months and two weeks later Marsha was said to be in complete possession of her faculties. Her doctors released her with the clothes she had arrived in, plus three prescriptions wadded up in her hand. After a few days at her mother's house she returned to Frank, where her family said she belonged.

Frank didn't exactly welcome Marsha back. He refused to sleep in the same room with her until he could determine her state of mind. He locked himself in the only bedroom and gave her the rest of the house.

"I have never felt so rejected in my entire life," Marsha cried. "Nobody has ever loved me, and at this point if somebody suddenly decided to treat me with respect, I just wouldn't know how to behave."

A week later she was visited by Martians whose green heads were bigger on one side than the other. Again they examined her with the softest hands she had ever felt, but they refused to take her back to Mars. After they left, Marsha went into a decline and, without explanation, cut her hair shorter on one side than the other. Frank thought that was odd. Then she cut all the sleeves off his shirts and the legs off his pants. "You better be glad I'm doing this to your clothes and not to you, Mister," she said.

That's when Frank knew for sure that nothing had changed. To escape his predicament he went out drinking with his construction buddies, stayed out all night, and spent his entire week's salary. That morning before going home, he headed straight for Uncle Bud's Place, where he had a $26. credit for having repaired a refrigerator. Bud had not yet opened his liquor store, but he allowed Frank inside anyway.

"Want a cup of coffee?" Bud asked.

"Something stronger," Frank answered.

Bud, realizing Frank was drunk, refused to honor his credit, so Frank staggered away empty-handed. Less than an hour later, however, enraged over having his credit denied, Frank returned with a sawed-off shotgun half-hidden under his shirt. Pointing the gun at Bud, he reached over the cash register and grabbed a fistful of bills. He threw a ten on the counter and took a bottle of Jack Daniels. "When you figure out how much I owe, just send me a bill or ask me to fix something else," he said, swaying toward the door. "You know where to find me."

Bud called the police. "You better come over here and straighten out Frank McAlister," he said. "In the condition he's in, he don't need to be out on the highways, besides that, he's got more than half my cash register in his pocket."

"I just wonder," Pearl said as she took her time decorating the church. "I just wonder what Frank's up to today. I wonder why he's on my mind."

FOUR

Marsha's family lived just outside Canton, Arkansas, but Frank's people lived in an East Texas town called More-hope. His mother was the only piano teacher in town. Once a beautiful woman, Miss Fane's face had fallen into a sour expression that had become more pronounced by the years. At one time she had been an expert gardener, but like her beauty, her green thumb eventually withered. At the height of her gardening years she had grown hollyhocks, lilies and hydrangeas in her front yard and vegetables and roses in the back. The vegetables, mostly corn and peas, she had sold on her porch or canned for winter. She had been famous, especially for her white corn, which was sweet and tender, and even though she shared her seeds with friends, their crops were never quite as good. Because of her uncanny ability to grow things she had served as president of the Morehope Garden Club for six consecutive years. "If she touches a seed it will sprout anywhere, even in the palm of your hand." That had been her gardening reputation until Pearl, pulled down by her husband's death, cast a gloom over the McAlister house and caused Miss Fane to lose interest in gardening forever.

During the Second World War, when Pearl's husband, Teddy, was sent overseas, she returned home to deliver his child. She moved back into her old room on the second floor of the Greek revival house her father had built and there she stayed while her mother taught piano and maintained the house and garden. In the spring of that year the birth of her son was followed within a week by her husband's untimely death.

When the postman delivered the black-edged envelope, Pearl, who had been loved for her high spirits and contagious laughter, was picking roses in the backyard while keeping an eye on her son sleeping in a basket. With her arms filled with roses, and a heart that was heavy from months of anticipation, she opened the envelope and read the message. "Killed in combat." The words leaped from the letter. Hurling the roses across the backyard, she watched them fall like drops of blood into the rows of corn. She stood before her sleeping son, took him into her arms and then, feeling as though the earth had swallowed her up, she fell to her knees. Little Teddy rolled from her arms and into the garden where the cut roses were hanging from the cornstalks.

Miss Fane, who happened to be staring out her bedroom window, witnessed the whole thing. "Oh, no," she said when her daughter fell face forward onto the grass, "if Pearl dies on us, what on earth will we do with that baby?"

In years to come Miss Fane would often recall that day. "I swear to God Almighty I thought Pearl was dead," she would remind Wanda Gay. "She looked dead. She felt dead. And for all practical purposes she *was* dead because she certainly hasn't come to life since. Not for very long anyway. I don't know what it will take to wake Pearl up again."

While sorrow pulled life out of her, Pearl placed Little Teddy in her mother's care while she slept or read or walked around wearing her late husband's bathrobe and Purple Heart. "She was forever sleepwalking in those first few weeks after Big Teddy's death," Miss Fane would remember. "How we ever kept up with her, I'll never know."

Wearing her husband's bathrobe, held together with

a laundry pin or Teddy's Purple Heart, Pearl had often sleepwalked in broad daylight. During a piano lesson she would sometimes wander through the house never bumping into the furniture or crashing into a wall. At times she would escape through the back door and walk all over town. Everyone said that she seemed to float rather than walk and at times she even spoke to old friends who happened to be in her path, but she never called them by their correct names. She also had no recollection of her meanderings by day or night.

If she didn't return by herself, Miss Fane would receive a call from someone who had seen Pearl at her father's grave, or wandering through what was left of the bodyshop where Albert had lived and repaired cars. Sometimes she would walk in circles around and around Albert's tin shed, retracing the ruts of his fast cars in the red clay. Sometimes she would lie in his lumpy bed and wish she could spend five more minutes with him, just five was all it would take to straighten out their differences. She was prepared to say anything to lessen her father's disappointment and anger. She was prepared to make any apology necessary to break her father's silence.

"How much longer can this go on?" Miss Fane had said. "I'm too old to be raising another child. Pearl's got to come to her senses."

On one of her sleeping walks through the two-story house, Pearl was awakened by her mother holding Teddy over the hot stove. "What are you doing?" she screamed.

"Stirring the soup, and teaching my pupils, and trying to feed your motherless child," Miss Fane said. "Meanwhile the garden needs watering and the house needs sweeping and the laundry is piling up."

At that moment Little Teddy stuck his fingers into the hot soup and began crying. "Give me my child," Pearl demanded. "It's time for me to be his mother now." She never walked in her sleep again, nor did she allow her mother to care for her son.

"Mother wants to boil my child alive," she told Wanda Gay.

"Mother wants to boil you right along with him, I'm sure," Wanda, a mother herself, replied.

"Mother has scalded my son's hand," Pearl told Reverend Stillwell, who had come to pray for her. "Fortunately, he will not be handicapped, not even scarred. Mother claimed she was trying to give him some nourishment, but she was actually trying to add him to the dinner."

"Not Miss Fane," the minister said.

"Oh, yes," Pearl added, "One of Daddy's cats disappeared the same way."

Reverend Stillwell moved Pearl's name to the top of his prayer list.

"Not only has Mother attempted to render my son into soup," Pearl told Miss Winnie, Morehope's retired English teacher, "she has lost interest in gardening. All day long the house is filled with music students banging on the piano. How would you like to live with that?"

"You are out of place here," Miss Winnie said. "Just like your grandmother Perdita. She didn't belong in this town and neither do you. It's time for you to go live someplace else."

"If I only knew where to go I'd leave," Pearl replied. "But I just don't know anything anymore. I seem to be frozen in one place."

"Pearl has completely lost her mind," Miss Fane told Wanda Gay. "She imagines things that are not true. That's what happens when you expect too much. When you put all your eggs in one basket and then the basket gets stolen, you are asking for a breakdown. Whether you know it or not you are beginning to fall apart. That's just the way some people are. Pearl, you see, wrapped her entire life around Big-Teddy-who-died-in-the-war. Now all she's got are memories and Little Teddy to keep her company."

While Pearl cared for her son and entertained her sorrow, her mother took on more piano students and continued to lose interest in her yard. Within a year the lawn developed bald spots. The flowers wilted and died. And the dry cornstalks rattling in the wind kept Miss Fane awake at night. Deciding she was too old to garden anymore, she bought three truckloads of gravel and paid to have it spread all over the yard. "Nothing will ever grow here again," she said, packing the gravel with her feet. "And I don't care."

Due to the condition of her yard, the garden club expelled her from membership. She said that she had lost her green thumb because Pearl's on-going depression had cast a gloom over her life.

"Do you remember when Pearl used to make us laugh?" she would ask Wanda Gay. "That seems like such a long time ago. Now all she does is read the encyclopedias to that boy of hers, and if she keeps on doing that she'll make a moron out of him. Infants don't need to hear what the encyclopedias have to say."

"I'm going to write that down, Mother," said Wanda Gay. She had recently started keeping a notebook of her mother's sayings. "I don't want anyone to forget what you just said, and I sure don't want anyone to forget that I agreed with you. Buying a child a set of encyclopedias before he's learned how to walk is not right. I have allowed my daughter to be a child, and I want her to go on being a child just as long as she wants to be one."

Wanda Gay's daughter, Demeris, was one year old when Little Teddy was born. "Unless you stop treating her like she's made of glass, you're going to have a baby on your hands for the rest of your life," Pearl once told her sister. "I'm determined not to have that problem."

As Pearl watched her son grow, she realized how much she depended on him to give her life a sense of stability. She also realized how much he favored Big Teddy. "Your father and I came from an entirely different time and place," she told him. "We may have even belonged to another race, one the world has forgotten all about.

There will never be anyone else quite like him. He was the best of all men."

The top floor of the McAlister house became Pearl's domain. Miss Fane never set foot there and before long Pearl had little desire to descend the stairs. "The first floor of this house is another world," she told her son. "We don't live there. That's mother's world, but we are required to visit it occasionally."

"I don't know what's wrong with Pearl," Wanda Gay had gone around saying. "I have always thought she was stronger than I because she was capable of going her own way, but now I question my former judgment."

"Big Teddy's death pulled her down," Miss Fane said. "After you get pulled down by death it's hard to pull yourself back up again. That's why I never allowed myself to get that close to Albert."

"Mother, that is so sensible," said Wanda Gay. "It has to be written down."

"And while you're at it," Miss Fane said, "you can write this down too: Pearl's problem started when she married a man she loved too much. You, Wanda Gay, will never have the same problem. That's one thing you can be thankful for."

FIVE

After Pearl had returned to Morehope to take up residence on the second floor of the old McAlister house, Wanda Gay said that her sister didn't know how lucky she was to be able to live at home all over again. Many years later on that long car trip to Canton, Arkansas, she would say the same thing: "Pearl is the luckiest human in the world. There are days when I'd give anything to have my old room back. Pearl not only has her old room, she's got my old room as well as Frank's old room. She has spread out all over the entire second floor and that's not right. What if I need to move back suddenly? What if we *are* able to get Frank out of jail and *he* has to move back suddenly? Where would we go? Thanks to Pearl we don't have a home anymore."

"If you didn't dislike your present situation so much you wouldn't always be talking about moving back," said Miss Fane as she studied the highway map by flashlight and Pearl exceeded the speed limit to clear her mind.

"I could have prevented this marital catastrophe of yours," Miss Fane ranted, "but you didn't listen to me, and now you're saddled with a man who has no ambition and no money and not a shred of hope for betterment. He hasn't even provided you with a half-way adequate house."

Wanda Gay hated her house and its location. "I blame my misfortunate living conditions on you," she often said

29

to her husband, Jerry Striker, who was called Sunday because he enjoyed resting. They had met in the first grade and had married shortly after graduation from high school. They rented a one-bedroom house with low ceilings and no dining room, and when their daughter Demeris approached her teens, Wanda Gay insisted on turning their bedroom over to her. "It's necessary to have your own bedroom during these tender years," she said.

Wanda and Jerry slept in the living room on a convertible sofa, which Wanda Gay was constantly having to reinforce with bricks and two-by-fours, owing to her husband's problem with his weight. "One day when we buy that house next to Mother, we'll have a bedroom again, and won't have to sleep on a couch," Wanda was forever saying.

"One day when we move into the house next to Grandmother," Demeris would reply, "I will have *my* own bedroom and won't have to borrow somebody else's. I hate borrowing bedrooms."

On the day of Frank's incarceration, Wanda Gay finally persuaded her husband to take out a loan and buy the house next door to Miss Fane. The Johnsons, who had lived there over twenty years and had been contemplating selling for the last seven, finally decided to go ahead and move into a smaller place. Before the papers were signed Wanda Gay stopped by the Methodist church to deliver the news to Pearl, who was slowly decorating the sanctuary, her annual contribution to her mother's piano recital.

By then, Pearl's *Frank feeling* had become more intense. "I'm too nervous today," she told Lefty. "I'm just going to throw these decorations together the best I can and not worry about it." She was having trouble holding things, especially scissors and cigarettes, and when she saw her sister entering the church she knew that her nerves were about to be tested.

In one proud breath Wanda Gay told Pearl that they were not only sisters but soon-to-be-neighbors.

"I'll kill myself if you move into that house," Pearl

said, hurling crepe paper and ribbon across the church. "How would you feel knowing you were responsible for that?"

"Pearl, I have always been a responsible human being," Wanda Gay argued. "*I* take after Mother."

"Oh, my dear, dear, Sister," Pearl said with feigned sympathy. "Please, don't go around town telling everyone that. Even though the entire county knows it already, I believe it would embarrass me to death if someone outside the family were to actually say it to my face."

"I am Mother made over," said Wanda Gay, "and I'm proud of it."

"Yes, I know you are." Pearl lit a Lucky Strike while backing her sister out the door. "But you must understand this: I can't be responsible for my actions, especially if I'm forced to spend more than an hour a week in the same room with you and Mother. I now know what Daddy went through all those years."

Pearl, throwing cigarettes, scissors, and keys, chased Wanda Gay down the sidewalk and back to her car idling on the curb. "Don't you ever come near me unless you have good news to report," Pearl shouted as Wanda Gay locked her doors.

Watching her sister drive away, Pearl was reminded of the time her father had banished her from his automobile graveyard, his mechanic's shop, and his life. Albert had taken an instant disliking to Big Teddy and after learning that his daughter was planning her wedding against his wishes, he had chased her out of the graveyard and across the railroad tracks. "I may be a cripple, but I can still move pretty fast when I need to," he shouted, throwing hubcaps at the daughter who was about to disappoint him.

SIX

Albert McAlister, Morehope's lame mechanic, died shortly after Pearl returned home to deliver her son. During the last months of his life he had not wanted to see anyone except his favorite customers, his barber, and his cats. He'd had nothing to say to his daughter who had not only married against his wishes but had become pregnant with what he called a "stranger's child."

"The institution of marriage is the Devil's invention," Albert had preached to his son, his customers, and his barber. "Marriage is senseless. Take it from me."

Because he preached against the vows of matrimony, upon his death many of the newcomers to Morehope didn't realize that he had a wife. "It came as quite a shock," said Imogene Wardlaw, "especially since I'm on the census board. I've been here five years and I knew that Albert had several women admirers, but I sure didn't know that he was married. I have always thought his wife was his landlady because they sometimes lived in the same house but not together. Isn't that right?"

"Well, I knew he was married," said her husband, "but I sure didn't know he was married to that piano teacher. A man like Albert too. That's almost unbelievable. You wonder how it happened."

Miss Fane first saw Albert when he came to help his father and brothers repair the roof of Judge Fane's house. She was sixteen years old and called by her first name,

Eugenia, and Albert was almost ten years her senior. Their eyes met while she was standing on the front lawn and he was on the roof. Not believing his eyes, Albert dropped his hammer and stood up. He had only dreamed of such beauty: long black hair, skin pale and translucent as alabaster, long tapering hands and fingers. But it was her delicate ankles that caused his knees to give way. He collapsed on the shingles and rolled off the roof, landing at Eugenia's feet.

She stood there, unmoved by what had happened, until he rolled over on his side and kissed her ankles. Then she ran screaming into the house and her mother, Perdita Ogletree-Fane, scrubbed her feet with hot water and strong detergent. "Don't tell anyone what he did," she begged her mother. "I could lose all my friends over this."

A few years later Albert, a tenor, turned up in the Methodist choir. Eugenia Fane was the organist and again their eyes often met. He thought she was the most beautiful woman in town, and she thought his appearance startling. His thin face was thrown off balance by a long sharp nose, and his eyes were deeply set. "He has the look of a crow from the side and a frog from the front," she told her girlfriends. All of them disagreed.

"He's totally unacceptable," Eugenia told her mother.

"And yet," said Perdita, "all your friends are madly in love with him. I'm sure it has something to do with the fact that he's a cripple."

Albert, lame from falling off the roof, hobbled around without complaining and without saying much to anyone. The girls said it was his almost impenetrable silence that intrigued them; his silence along with his limp and his thick black hair, which was long for the day and always appeared, even when freshly combed, to have been slept on and tangled by admiring hands. He rarely spoke except to say hello, and all of the young girls counted the number of times he had acknowledged them with that one word of greeting, sometimes accompanied by a wink, sometimes just a squint from both eyes. Because he was so admired by her friends, Eugenia Fane suddenly began to take notice. When Albert opened his mouth to sing, everyone listened, especially Eugenia.

He was almost thirty when they married, and without a dime of savings. His lack of money didn't bother his wife then, but later on it did. "Albert had no concern for the value of a dollar," she told her children at her husband's wake. Frank had just arrived, improperly dressed according to his mother, who was trying to ignore him. "Money just ran through Albert's fingers," she continued, glaring at her only son. "Loose change and loose women, that's all he thought about and I'm looking at somebody else who has the same problem. Because of me we can afford to bury Albert."

"Because of you, Mother, we are all standing here today," said Wanda.

"You make me want to hit you," said Pearl.

"Because of me, Albert's got a coffin to spend the rest of eternity in," said Miss Fane.

"Because of you, Mother, we've got a family," said Wanda Gay.

"Don't you have a mind of your own?" asked Frank.

"Pearl," said Wanda Gay, "Frank's talking to you. He's asking you a question. He wants to know if you have a mind left. I don't know how to answer that question right now."

"Wanda Gay, you make me want to hit you for being so stupid," Pearl said, "but it wouldn't do either of us any good."

"Because of me, Albert had a purpose in life." Miss Fane raised her voice to upstage her daughters' quarrel. "I gave him a reason to live. It's not my fault that he didn't appreciate what I had to offer."

"I have always wanted to know something," Frank said. "Why *did* you marry Daddy anyway?"

"She needed a nice person to whip," said Pearl.

"That is most assuredly not true, Pearl," said Miss Fane, shaking a dry handkerchief in Pearl's face.

"Pearl, that is most assuredly not true," said Wanda Gay, digging in her purse to find a handkerchief to shake.

"Some people have to have a slave," said Frank. "And it's usually the nice people who need to be bullied. That was Daddy's weakness. He needed to be a slave."

"Albert was not a slave to anybody, Frank," Miss Fane said over the closed casket. "He was a handyman, and that's why I married him. Now get the facts straight because I might not be around forever to remind you. Albert could fix anything from your roof to your radio, and I thought it would be convenient to marry a handyman, but I sure found out different. You don't *marry* a handyman, you *hire* a handyman. Unfortunately, this is not something that you can tell somebody and hope they will profit by it. For example, look what happened to Wanda Gay. She married half a handyman." Miss Fane pointed a gloved finger into Wanda Gay's face. "Now don't deny it. I know you did, and you know it too. At least, I had the sense to marry a full-fledged handyman. It's not my fault that he didn't finish out his life."

"I wonder what really killed Daddy?" Pearl asked.

"Pneumonia," said Miss Fane in a calm voice that betrayed her need to scream. "Double pneumonia. I already told you that once."

"Pneumonia" was written on the death certificate, but the nurses at the county hospital had a different opinion. They said that Miss Fane aggravated Albert to death along with the entire hospital staff from the chief dietitian right on down to the admissions clerk. "She did nothing but run everybody ragged," Ethel Petigo, the head nurse, had said. "She expected us to wait on her as if she were the one who was dying. That woman can ask for more glasses of water than anybody I ever knew."

Albert had been a soft-spoken man, a lover of animals, and the best mechanic in Morehope. His automobile grave-yard covered four acres of land on the outskirts of town, and his mechanic's shed was large enough to contain three cars. There Albert spent his most contented years, sharing his meals with a few special customers and eight, long-haired tom cats. Miss Fane, who claimed to be allergic to cats as well as the smell of motor oil, kept her husband at a distance, and eventually Albert took up residence at his place of business.

"I am allergic to odors of all kinds," she had reminded her children as they stood over Albert's coffin. "Odors just about make me want to die on the spot. That's why when Albert took up mechanics, I was thoughtful enough to provide him with his very own bedroom, his very own bathroom, and his very own entrance to the house. But he seemed to prefer sleeping in that drafty old bodyshop with all those cats and God only knows what or who else. He did it for spite too, just to embarrass me. That was the mean streak coming out of him."

"Meanness is something you can't fool Mother on." Frank leaned on his father's casket.

"You can too," Wanda Gay replied, thinking she was defending her role model.

"When it comes to meanness," Pearl added, "Mother sure knows her business."

"Go ask my piano pupils," said Miss Fane, struggling to speak in a low voice. "They will tell you how sweet I am. And they will also tell you that I am very lenient on them. There's not a mean bone in my body."

"No there isn't," said Frank. "Only hard ones."

"You're the *best* piano teacher in Morehope," said Wanda Gay.

"You're the *only* piano teacher in Morehope," said Pearl.

"And *therefore* the best," said Frank.

Miss Fane hated the word *therefore*, and had always accused Frank of using it against her. "Frank, I will say this one more time, and that's it," she said. "I am not the best because I'm the only one. I'm the best because I'm the best. There's no *therefore* to it."

Frank turned his back on her and stared at his father's coffin. Miss Fane had insisted on keeping it closed. "Frank, I know what you're thinking and the answer is no," Miss Fane said. "Don't you dare do so much as crack the lid on Albert's coffin. I don't want to see him, not ever again. I have my own memories, and they are just fine. I don't want to remember him the way he is."

SEVEN

While taping ribbons and carnations on the sides of the church pews, Pearl, forgetting her *Frank feeling* for a while, remembered the pleasant years she had spent with her father and wished they could be relived. Together they had spent hours searching through the automobile graveyard looking for used parts that could be used once again. They had looked for carburetors, and generators, and axle rods, or mufflers, or spare tires, or rearview mirrors that Albert could then use to repair his customers' cars.

Holding her *Frank feeling* at bay, she continued decorating the pews while thinking of her father, the hours she had spent rolling cigarettes for him, and the practice it had taken to perfect her technique.

"Daddy always said if the tobacco wasn't evenly distributed, the flavor wasn't the same," Pearl told Lefty. "He was right too. Every morning I'd roll enough cigarettes to last him the entire day. He said mine were better than his and better than Frank's too."

She recalled the long walks they had taken together through the graveyard of wrecked cars. From week to week the size and the shape of the place had changed, sometimes drastically. Albert was constantly buying new wrecks to add to what was already there. He was constantly having to search for new paths through the demolished or rundown cars. Often they would be deep within the wreckage and he would pretend to be lost to test his daughter's sense of direction. "Which way out? I don't believe I know," he'd say, turning around and around. As if he were blind, Pearl would lead him by the hand in and out of the maze of wrecked automobiles and trucks until she stumbled upon a path that led them to Cedar Creek, which bisected the graveyard. From there she would follow the creek on its circuitous route through the wrecks, and along the way Albert would point to various smashed cars and tell her who had owned them and whether or not the accident had been fatal.

Sometimes he pointed to a 1935 Chevrolet with a crushed top, which he left as a reminder. "Flat as a pancake," he would say. "You and Frank were very lucky to get out of that alive."

In spite of the car accident that had almost taken their lives, Pearl continued to feel a sense of tranquility at the automobile graveyard. A purposeful calm that had never been present at home, not even when her father was still living there, was evident among the wreckage. She had felt comfortable in her father's tin mechanics shop filled with tools, cats, and the smell of motor oil that had stained the earth with rainbows. At her mother's house all was nervous energy, and piano students, and the ticking metronome.

"I wonder how much longer mother can go on teaching piano," Pearl said to Lefty, who was resting on a pew. "Her students perform the same old pieces year after year. I'm so tired of listening to them I could scream, and if Mother actually listened she'd be tired of them too."

"No wonder your daddy didn't like living at home," said Lefty.

"Poor Daddy," Pearl said. "I was just thinking about him. There was hardly a day when a student wasn't banging on the piano. But that was only one of the many reasons why he went to live in his body shop, Lefty, surely everybody realizes that by now. All I know is if Daddy were still alive, I'd be living down at the automobile graveyard right along with him and all his cats. I'd be there whether he wanted me or not, and we'd be replacing mufflers and fan belts and rotating tires and changing oil and eating canned beans. We'd be buying old cars and making them over and searching through the wreckage and pretending to be lost. Of course, I'd have to listen to him complain about Teddy, but that would certainly be better than putting up with Mother every day, I can promise you that."

"You ever wonder where you'd be right now if your husband had made it through the war?" Lefty asked.

Had it not been for the sincerity in Lefty's voice, Pearl would have been shocked by his question. "Why yes, Lefty, I do wonder that," she said. Her voice drifted far away as if traveling back in time. "I think about Teddy constantly, but now during certain times of the year I think about him in a different way. There are times, particularly in the winter when the world is still and very quiet, I have a lot of trouble believing that he's dead."

EIGHT

Little Teddy was twelve years old the year of his uncle's self-incarceration. More than a decade later, when he traveled to Brazil to claim Frank's body and bring it home, the tropical heat was to remind him of that unusually hot spring and his grandmother's accusation that Frank had deliberately planned the robbery to conflict with her piano recital.

On that day in the spring of 1955, Sam Sticks's wife, who had taken it upon herself to notify the family whether Frank wanted it or not, had been trying to call Miss Fane all morning, but she had been too busy to answer the telephone. "I do believe that's bad news calling," she said every time it rang. "Bad news and bad weather always go together, and for that reason I forbid anyone to go near that ringing telephone. I don't need a setback, not today I don't."

In the early afternoon, with the telephone ringing in the background, Little Teddy practiced his recital piece, a Bach etude way beyond his ability, which his grandmother had chosen especially for him. While he practiced against the ringing telephone, Miss Fane, with Wanda Gay at her side, visited the beauty parlor. Their hair was cut, curled, and combed into tiny ringlets. Only Helen of the House of Helen could please them. "She understands our hair." Wanda Gay repeated Miss Fane, and Miss Fane repeated Wanda Gay. They always left the House of Helen with the same cut and curl but not the same color. Miss Fane's hair was frosty blue and Wanda's was then jet black.

When Miss Fane returned home, Little Teddy was still practicing his recital piece. He had not yet played it all the way through without a mistake. "Start over!" Miss Fane shouted as she came into the house. (She was stuffing Kleenex into her collar to catch the perspiration.) "Start over until you get it right!" The phone was ringing again, but she didn't care. Ignoring it, she stood behind her grandson and covered his eyes with a damp Kleenex while he played the etude yet again. "Piano playing is no different than touch typing," she said. "The more you look at your fingers, the more mistakes you're apt to make. One of these years I'm going to establish a new rule: all recitals will be played blindfolded."

"Well, I hope this isn't the year," said her grandson. He was burning up. The temperature was in the high nineties for the fifth day, and there wasn't an electric fan in the house. Pearl had taken them all to the Methodist church. She had already decorated the studio piano with pine cones, cedar, and white carnations, and Lefty Simmons had vacuumed out the sanctuary.

"You know, Lefty, there's nothing else to do," she said, "but I'm not ready to go home. Mother's nerves will be on edge. They always are on recital days, so I'd just as soon stay here until the last minute."

Lefty put away his janitorial supplies and Pearl, breathing much easier, stretched out on one of the pews and took a nap. Two hours before the recital she woke up with Miss Winnie Barlow staring down at her.

"It's disgraceful," said Miss Winnie, Pearl's retired English teacher, "to assume a recumbent position upon a church pew."

"Miss Winnie," said Pearl, "the church is filled with peace and tranquility. That's what you used to say when I was in your class. Now, after all these years, I'm finally taking your word for it."

"Your clothes!" said Miss Winnie. "Pearl, when is this phase going to pass? What can we do to help you?"

Pearl sat up and lit a Lucky Strike.

"Smoking in the sanctuary!" exclaimed Miss Winnie. "Pearl, when are you going to wake up and be yourself again?"

"Yes, it's true," Pearl said, "I'm wearing my dead husband's clothes, and I'm smoking in the sanctuary, but who are we going to notify about this, Miss Winnie, the fire department or the Lord? This afternoon I can be perfectly comfortable with either!"

"You speak with too many exclamation marks," said Miss Winnie as she fled the church.

In years to come, when Pearl looked back on this day, she thought of Miss Winnie, who had also taught Frank and Wanda Gay and she wondered if their old English teacher had ever been in love. Standing over Frank's ebony coffin she wondered the same thing about her brother and her sister but not about herself. She had the satisfaction of knowing that she had been in love, of knowing that she had tried to fall in love again. "It's harder the second time than the first, because you're trying harder," she admitted to herself.

"I wonder," she often said to Wanda Gay as they sat on the wedding porch and listened to the creaking of the old swing. "I wonder, is it possible to have more than one great love in your lifetime? After you've had one great love it seems to me it's impossible to have another one. Do you think I'm right, Sister?"

Wanda Gay rarely reworded her answer. "Sister, it depresses me to hear you talk this way. Why don't you put this worn-out topic to rest once and for all. You already know my opinion: there's no such thing as love. You just have to get used to each other. Sometimes it takes a long time and sometimes it doesn't."

NINE

When Pearl returned home from the Methodist church, Little Teddy, blindfolded with a nylon scarf, was still practicing his recital piece, and Miss Fane, dressed in a pink lace blouse and a long potesea skirt, was racing to the telephone, which was ringing once again.

"I don't know which is worse, that boy's piano playing or this telephone," she said, searching her purse for a candy. "One of them has got to stop."

She picked up the receiver and pressed it against her leg so the caller wouldn't hear her scolding her grandson. "Lay off the hard pedal! I've got bad nerves, you know. Does anybody ever stop to think about that?"

Then, protecting her hair and make-up, she held the telephone well away from her tight curls and powdered face. "Will you hold just a moment longer, please," she said sweetly. "I'm having a discussion with my grandson right now."

Pressing the receiver against her leg again, she raised her voice. "Little Teddy, as God is my only witness, I'll slap you into next week for playing everything forte. Now will you stop it or will you force me to get ugly? Not everything is written forte. Follow the designated dynamics, or go outside, I don't care which."

While Miss Fane was shouting at Little Teddy, Pearl entered through the kitchen door. During that period of her life she still had a war-bride look about her. In her

44

clothes closet the 1940s were still living. Blouses with shoulder pads, fitted jackets, and straight skirts had been her everyday look. For many years, however, she had taken to wearing pants of all kinds, including a pair of Big Teddy's that swallowed her.

"Pants are not to be worn in public places!" Miss Fane abruptly turned her attention from Little Teddy to Pearl. "How many times have I told you not to go down to the church dressed like that. A decent woman doesn't need to wear pants to decorate the pews. One of these days somebody will see you and criticize you, and put your name on a public prayer list, and I'm talking about the one that's published in the newspaper. Don't you ever leave this house looking like that or you'll lose your reputation."

"I've already lost so much," Pearl said. "It really doesn't matter if I lose any more or not."

It was an hour before the recital. Pearl sat down at the kitchen table and smoked a Lucky Strike, Big Teddy's brand. After a few minutes she stubbed it out. "I don't think I'll dress up tonight," she said just to aggravate her mother.

"If you did, I'd die from shock," Miss Fane spoke into the telephone and to her daughter at the same time. "I would drop dead on the spot if you suddenly took an interest in your appearance."

"Then maybe I *will* dress up," Pearl replied with a devilish smile. "I'll dress up just for you, Mother."

"Will you hold a moment longer please?" Miss Fane spoke sweetly but did not give her caller a chance to reply. "I'm talking to one of my daughters now." Then she covered the mouthpiece with her hand and addressed Pearl in a sharp voice. "When was the last time you wore anything besides pants, anyway?"

"Slacks," Pearl corrected. "They're called slacks."

Miss Fane did not answer back. She was listening to her caller while fanning her face with a handkerchief. The air in the house was still and blistering hot, and Pearl could feel her mother's agitation infiltrating the room.

Suddenly, Miss Fane turned pale; she struggled for her breath or to utter a sound, Pearl could not tell which. At that moment her *Frank feeling* returned in full force. "This is just like waiting for a tornado to hit," she said, lighting another Lucky. She had known that anticipation before a storm many times in her life, and she knew she would know it many times to come. "This is something you never get used to," she said, watching her mother's hands trembling.

Miss Fane's fingers raced over her throat and shoulders as if searching for something that was stinging her. Then she slipped a piece of candy in her mouth.

"Bad news," Pearl said. "Has to be Frank. He's the only one who can make Mother's hands shake like that."

"I happen to be a sugar diabetic invalid!" Miss Fane screamed into the receiver which she held away from her face. "I have a severe heart murmur, and a bad back coupled with high blood pressure and raw nerves. I am not, I repeat, AM NOT allowed to receive information of this kind. It could kill me on the spot. Somebody has to prepare me to face these things gradually. Somebody," she pointed to Pearl, "has fallen down on *her* job."

For a moment Pearl felt a sense of relief. It was always difficult living with her mother up until the initial outburst. When she had been blackballed from the garden club, Miss Fane had harbored her anger for four days before exploding at the postman for not delivering any mail. Those were four hard, long, agonizing days of nothing but waiting, Pearl remembered. At least we're getting an early start this time.

Suddenly Miss Fane threw the receiver to the floor as if it had turned hot in her hands. "Frankie's a good boy, and we love him," she said. The energy was leaving her voice. "In spite of two or three bad faults I haven't been able to do anything about, he is still a good boy. Oh, why did God let this happen in my lifetime. Couldn't

He have put this off just a little bit longer. I don't have much time left anyway."

Little Teddy removed his blindfold, and Pearl leaned in her chair for a better view. From opposite ends of the hall their eyes met at the telephone table where Miss Fane stood motionless except for beads of perspiration rolling down her powdered face. All the color applied to her cheeks and lips seemed to fade instantly. Gasping for her breath, she gazed at a mother of pearl cameo, the only ring she ever wore. "May the dear Lord take me tonight," she groaned. "Frankie's been thrown in jail, and he needs us bad. The family must come together now. I insist!"

"I knew something was wrong," said Pearl. "I've had one of those feelings all day."

"Why don't you let your feelings be known?" said Miss Fane. "You could have prepared me for this."

"I wouldn't dare try to prepare you for anything," Pearl said, filing her nails. "I wouldn't know how." She was sick with worry about her brother, but refused to give her mother the satisfaction of knowing it.

"All this is Marsha's fault," Miss Fane said. Her voice was very weak.

"First it was God's fault," Pearl said. "Now it's Marsha's fault. Pretty soon it's going to be my fault, but everybody who has any sense left knows that Frank's problems started right here." Pearl pointed to her mother.

That made Miss Fane livid. While polishing the cameo on her skirt, she stood there glaring at her daughter. "Let me tell you something right now," she said, suddenly regaining her strength. "At the age of thirty-six you have discovered too much joy in becoming plain-spoken to a fault. I've caught on to this trick of yours."

"I've caught on to you too, Mother," Pearl replied. "You never thought I would but I did a long time ago. All you want to do is gripe. Since early this morning you have blamed me for thirteen things, including burning the toast and sugaring your coffee, so why should you stop now?"

"I wouldn't think of stopping now because thirteen is an unlucky number." Miss Fane spoke with her teeth clenched. "I wouldn't wish bad luck on anybody, including my own children. And while we're on the subject let me say this: since the first of the year, all you have studied is how to aggravate everybody in sight, how to stir up discontent in yourself and others, and how to take your time doing things you used to be fast at. I'm not the only one who's noticed this change in you either."

"I didn't know people around here knew how to take notice," Pearl said, making aggressive use of the ash tray. "May the dear Lord take you tonight, Mother." She raised her voice so Miss Fane would be sure to hear every word. "It would do my heart good to see you out of your misery."

"Ah ha," Miss Fane said. "Now the truth comes out. Now I know why you sugared my coffee this morning. Knowing I'm a diabetic invalid, you were trying to finish me off."

"That may have been my unconscious motive, indeed," Pearl confessed.

"Shame on you for attempting to bring disaster upon yourself. Where would you be without me? What would you have to get up for?"

"Plenty," said Pearl, without raising her voice.

"I forbid you to speak that way in·my presence," said Miss Fane, shaking her cameo in Pearl's face.

"Forgive me, please, for putting you in such a bad mood." Pearl pretended to beg. "If I had come home in time to answer the telephone, I could have kept this bad news from touching you. And if I had not run off with all the electric fans, you wouldn't be on the verge of a heat stroke. Or would you?"

"How dare you stand there straightfaced and call attention to your own shortcomings before I've had a chance to do so," Miss Fane protested. "You are once again guilty of depriving me of my duty as a mother."

"You think I don't know that, I guess," Pearl said, but not loud enough for her mother to hear.

Still glaring, Miss Fane picked up the telephone and called Wanda Gay. At that moment Wanda was standing over her thirteen-year-old daughter and forcing her to play her recital piece one more time. Wanda Gay, already dressed for the occasion, was wearing a cocktail suit of pink rayon, with shoes and purse dyed to match and a sweetheart corsage pinned stemside down. Short white gloves completed her outfit.

"Wanda Gay," said Miss Fane. "Tell that sweet Demeris that the tempo of tonight's recital is going to be drastically accelerated. Tell her not to worry because nobody around here will know the difference anyway, and while you're at it, prepare her for the fact that I plan to use a metronome to speed things along. In fact, I intend to set it two or three notches faster on every piece because we've got to leave for Arkansas just as soon as possible. Frank's in jail, and Marsha's what put him there, and we've got to make it out of town before everybody in Morehope finds out about this. I figure we can go and come back in a day and a night without anybody missing us. And when the people of Canton see what a decent family Frank comes from they'll know right off that a mistake has been made."

"I agree with your every word, Mother," said Wanda Gay.

"I knew you would," said Miss Fane.

"I love Frank as much as anybody else," Wanda Gay continued. "But for some reason or other he wants to disgrace us in the eyes of absolutely everybody we know. How would we ever be able to hold the family together without you, Mother?"

"One day you'll have to," said Miss Fane. "And that day might not be too far away. That's why I'm training you to take my place. Somebody's got to be the mortar between the bricks. Right now that somebody is me, and pretty soon that somebody will be you."

"Oh, Mother, I'll never be able to fill your shoes,"

cried Wanda Gay as she rearranged the ribbons in her daughter's hair.

"Oh yes you will," said Miss Fane. "One day I'll take off this cameo ring and hand it over to you, and you know what that means. I inherited it from my mother, Perdita Ogletree-Fane, who inherited it from her mother, Sarah Eliza Ogletree, who inherited it from her mother, whose name I forget, and you'll inherit it from me. After I give it up, it is my intention to lie down and die."

"Promises, promises," said Pearl.

"Oh Mother," said Wanda Gay, gripping the telephone with her chin and shoulder. "You know how much I love that ring. I have written down its entire genealogy in your very own words." Holding gloved hands in front of her, she wondered if she would wear the ring on her left hand or her right hand. She wondered if it would need to be resized or if it would be a perfect fit.

In years to come Demeris would wonder the same thing, and Wanda Gay would curse herself for not having had another child. "It's important to have a choice of heirs," she would say to Pearl during their last spring. "Demeris doesn't care as much about this ring as she ought to. If I turn it over to her, that cheap lazy husband of hers is liable to sell it. And for that reason, Pearl, I don't want my fat, destructive daughter inheriting this house or anything in it. What with all those monsters she's given birth to, the floor boards would be ripped up inside a week and all of Mother's fine furniture would be soiled by dirty hands and chewed on by all those nasty-smelling dogs they live with."

TEN

During the second half of her life, Pearl was to be haunted by the ticking of a phantom metronome that kept her in constant motion. The ticking followed her from room to room and from street to grocery store to post office and bank. Wherever she went she often walked to the accompaniment of the ticking, first fast then slow. Her steps would quicken to keep pace or settle into a moderate tempo, an adagio perhaps or a long retard, which would suddenly give way to vivace, or allegro. "With spirit, with spirit," she would sometimes hear her mother shouting above the ticking. At first, thinking she was losing her mind, she would search outside herself for the source. Determined to find some logical cause for the almost constant ticking, she examined all the clocks and mechanical devices liable to go off automatically. Eventually she was forced to admit, but only to herself, that the ticking was in her mind. It pulsated through her veins and caused her to tap her foot at the most inappropriate times: at Frank's funeral, or at the commencement exercises when her son delivered the valedictory address, or, often as not, her foot would tap the accelerator of her Ford, causing it to jerk along in uneven spurts of high speed. When she least expected it, the ticking would start, rattling her nerves until she became temporarily accustomed to the sound and rhythm. Only when she had grown dependent on it for company would the mysterious metronome change rhythms abruptly or even worse, stop ticking altogether, leaving behind a sense of loss and emptiness, a deathly silence that drove Pearl to turn on the radio, television, and stereo in order to drive away the silence. She would sometimes walk through the house slamming all the windows and doors or throwing pots and pans onto the floor, or breaking bowls and vases that had been in the family for generations, anything to alleviate the sudden burst of silence that penetrated her like a cold breath. If the silence continued for days, she would eventually drive it away behind the wheel of her Ford. "Time to blow soot out of the engine," she would say, speeding through town on her way to the freeway, where the highway patrol, who knew to keep an eye out for her car, would stop her, issue a warning, and then follow her back home to the McAlister house. Eventually she would fall into bed and sleep until the ticking would again fill her with the desire to keep moving, and then the longing for a silence she could endure.

"After having lived with a real metronome ticking all day long for so very many years, it's hard to turn it off," Pearl explained in a letter to her grandson studying at the state university. "Tell that to your learned father who has such faith in your future and tell me what he says. Ask the doctor, my son, if he thinks it's abnormal to hear an almost constant ticking, ticking, ticking in many different speeds, first fast, then slow, then moderate, then slow, and then fast again. Tell him that I am unable to listen to music of any kind without hearing mother's metronome. I will be very anxious to receive the doctor's reply."

Often after a spell of silence the ticking would suddenly start again, and Pearl would glimpse her mother's piano students traipsing in and out of the living room or sitting on the Queen Anne chairs or the intricate parquet floor. Imagining them still coming and going lessened the loneliness of her last days and gave her much to talk or write about. The phantom students played the same old pieces Pearl had heard all her life, but it was the metronome which rang out the loudest and could be heard over the fortes, the hard pedal, and the diesel trucks groaning up the street.

Miss Fane's metronome was the loudest anyone had ever heard. She had liked it that way, especially when needing to speed up a lesson or a recital. "Frank was the only member of our family Mother ever got into a rush over," Pearl would write, first to her son and then her grandson, sometimes confusing one with the other. "When he was in jail that time, Mother told us to get ready for the speediest piano recital on record. And that's exactly what it was."

ELEVEN

The recital, the last one Pearl would ever attend, was held on a Friday evening, and according to Miss Fane it would be the last recital she would ever live through. She had said that about the last five recitals and everyone was convinced she would go on saying it for many years to come.

"Frank is waiting for us to save him," she had whispered to Wanda Gay as they entered the back door of the church. "That's why I'm determined to finish this recital fast."

Starting fifteen minutes early, Miss Fane sat behind the piano and wound up her metronome as tight as it would go. Then she instructed Donna Wiggley to begin at once. On the first chord, Donna's family and friends, all standing outside the church, rushed through the front door and scrambled to find a vacant pew. By the time they had settled themselves, Donna had played a page and a half and hardly anyone realized it except her mother, who was furious.

"I'm going to find another piano teacher for my daughter," said Mrs. Wiggley. "I swear I am. I don't care if I have to drive fifty miles. Eugenia Fane, or McAlister, or whatever we're supposed to call her, just won't do."

"Next!" Miss Fane shouted while Donna was still taking her bow.

"Why is she rushing my daughter off the stage?" said

Mrs. Wiggley, aiming her kodak. "I haven't taken a picture yet. I tell you I'm going to have that woman's ugly wrinkled neck before this recital's over."

"I hope not," said her four-year-old son.

"Next!" Miss Fane repeated, with a perturbed look on her face.

Billy Womack took his place at the piano, and before Donna made her final exit Miss Fane started the metronome at a faster speed.

"Who ever heard of using a metronome at a recital," Mrs. Womack said to her husband. "Has Eugenia Fane McAlister lost her mind?"

"That's too fast," said Billy. He could be heard all over the church.

"Our son is right," Mrs. Womack said to her husband. "The tempo is much too fast."

"Billy, don't you dare argue with me at a time like this," whispered Miss Fane as she smiled sweetly and sniffed the purple orchid her pupils had presented her. Billy's recital piece was called "Polka Dot Polka." "This piece," Miss Fane announced to the audience, "cannot be played too fast. In fact, the faster it's played the better it sounds."

Billy broke out in a cold sweat. His fingers trembled on the keyboard, and although he made numerous mistakes, he didn't stop.

While he took his bow Miss Fane allowed her eyes to drift over the half-filled church. There were five groups of people, with lots of space between each group. "Everybody's sitting so far apart because nobody knows how to get along anymore," she told Cissy Farrell as she sat down at the piano. "What a shame that people find it necessary to express their hatred at such an occasion. If we had more time, I'd get up and tell everyone where to sit and who to sit with and what to say."

Cissy began her recital piece, made a mistake on the second page, and started over. "We don't have time for you to start over," Miss Fane whispered with a serious smile on her face.

"Mother wants me to play it through without a mistake," Cissy said, her fingers racing over the keyboard. "If I do, she'll give me a dollar."

"Some people will do anything for money," Miss Fane whispered to her eleven-year-old pupil. "I suppose you're one of them."

"Yes, I am," said Cissy, refusing to take her eyes off the sheet music.

"Well," Miss Fane whispered, "I shudder to think of the kind of woman you will grow up to become."

Cissy messed up again and was about to start all over for the second time when Miss Fane jerked the first two pages off the music rack, and Cissy, forced to continue from where she left off, finished the sonata with tears in her eyes.

"What a little capitalist you are," Miss Fane said as Cissy stood up to take her bow.

In the back of the church Pearl, dressed in a pair of white slacks and one of Big Teddy's navy blue blazers, leaned against the wall and smoked. She had a faraway look in her eyes, and Miss Fane knew she was thinking about her late husband. She shot Pearl hard stares. Pearl shot them back. "No I will not put this cigarette out," Pearl mouthed slowly to her mother. "Not until Little Teddy has finished playing."

Miss Fane gave Pearl a serious smile and Pearl returned it.

She had already told her son not to look at his grandmother while he played. "Everybody who looks at her messes up," she had said. "So whatever you do, don't look up, and don't listen if she starts talking to you. She loves for her pupils to make mistakes because then she has an excuse to fuss."

Teddy made his entrance from the side room and everyone in the church gasped. At the last minute he had changed from his tuxedo into his Little League uniform.

"You are not properly dressed," Miss Fane hissed at her grandson. "How can you expect to perform with sensitivity if you're not attired for the occasion."

"I'm more comfortable in my Little League uniform," Teddy whispered without looking at his grandmother. Then he started playing.

"Don't take the repeats," his grandmother whispered. "Frank's waiting for us."

The etude was in three-quarter time, and Teddy, determined to ignore the metronome, started the piece at his own tempo. That pleased Pearl. She leaned against the back wall of the church and closed her eyes.

In her heart she was back on the army base, waltzing with Big Teddy at the officer's club. He was in uniform and she was wearing what she called her Ginger Rogers dress.

I wonder what ever happened to that beautiful dress, she thought as she watched herself dancing with her late husband. I wonder where it is now? She could see the officer's club as if it were a set from a forties musical in which she and Big Teddy were starring. They had been the best dancers on the army base, and had even given lessons to the other officers and their wives.

How did I learn to dance so well? Pearl wondered as her son continued at his own tempo in spite of the infernal ticking of Miss Fane's metronome. I wonder if I could still do it? If I could find that dress I know I could.

Suddenly, too abruptly for Pearl, her son finished the waltz he had been practicing all day. He finished without a mistake, and Pearl, not quite ready for the music to stop, was jarred back to the present moment. When she opened her eyes, Jerome Gasset, the pharmacist who had been trying to court her, was staring over his shoulder.

"I will not look at that odious man," she told herself, her lips subtly mouthing the words as she thought them.

She cast her eyes to the other side of the church and there on the back pew was another suitor, Lonnie Somerall, the high school math teacher. He had been in love with her for years. Their eyes met and Pearl quickly looked away.

"He's unctuous," she thought, again slightly mouthing the words. "Everywhere I go there's someone staring at me with *intentions*. I am so tired of being stared at with *intentions*."

She turned abruptly and left the church while Demeris, who was to play the "Moonlight Sonata," took her cousin's place at the piano.

"Pearl never stays to hear Demeris play," Wanda Gay whispered to Sunday, who was sound asleep. "She just hates our daughter, I know she does. I don't know why she doesn't come right out and say so."

Demeris began at a very slow tempo, in spite of the metronome ticking away on top of the piano. "Faster," Miss Fane kept whispering. "We've got to get out of here." And Demeris, unlike her cousin, could not disregard the measured ticking, so she resigned herself to Miss Fane's accelerated tempo.

"Not a mistake," Wanda whispered to Sunday when Demeris was taking her bow, but Sunday was still sleeping. "You have slept through one of the most wonderful moments of my life." Wanda Gay pressed a sharp elbow into her husband's side.

"I wasn't sleeping." Sunday slowly lifted his head. "I was just resting my eyes." He was wearing his Texaco uniform with his name, Jerry "Sunday" Striker, embroidered in red on his shirt pocket. He had three dress suits hanging in his closet, but he never wore any of them because they were too small. He now weighed 289 pounds and Wanda Gay often refused to occupy the sofa bed with him, sleeping instead on a reclining chair.

"I don't know what I'm going to do with you," she whispered as Miss Fane's next pupil began playing.

"I'm easy to please," Sunday said, only half opening his eyes. "Take me home and give me something to eat. That's all it takes."

While Jackie Hemphill struggled through her recital

piece, Miss Fane kept glancing at her watch. "Where-is-Pearl?" she mouthed to Wanda Gay, who shrugged her shoulders.

Pearl, ready for the recital to be over, was sitting on the steps of the church smoking and talking to Lefty, who was rolling a cigarette with one hand.

"I hate to be stared at, Lefty," Pearl said. "I hate a man who doesn't know how to dance too. Jerome Gasset can't waltz worth a damn. That's why I refused to go out with him again. Lonnie Somerall, the math teacher, can add in his brain but has two left feet, and Hank Best has only one arm. How can a woman dance with a man who has one arm?"

"You wouldn't be prejudiced toward the handicapped, would you?" Lefty held up his right arm, the hand of which was missing.

"I'm not prejudiced at all," Pearl said as she finished rolling Lefty's cigarette. "I'm practical. At least you have an arm to hold on to. Hank didn't even have that. I was stuck with an empty sleeve, and you cannot be led by an empty sleeve, Lefty. Remember that. You have a great deal to be thankful for."

"You should have married that rich man that time," Lefty said. "You'd have been fixed for life with him."

"He was handsome, all right," Pearl said, "but there was something odd about him that bothered me. On our third date he proposed. But he said that we could only live together six or seven months out of the year. The rest of the time his work kept him in Chicago. He was never able to explain exactly what he did nor why he couldn't have a wife with him."

"He had him a woman or two up there is my guess," said Lefty. "Best you didn't get mixed up with that."

Inside the church a piano duet was being played by the Desoto twins. "Frank and I played this duet one year," Pearl remembered. "At the last minute we decided to exchange parts and made a mess out of the whole thing. Mother was humiliated, of course. You should have seen her face up close, Lefty. I have never seen a nastier expression. After that we were not allowed to take part in any more recitals."

"Your boy's in the same fix," Lefty said. "That baseball uniform has finished him off. His recital days is over."

"I'm sure that's what he had in mind," Pearl said. "Mother will never forgive him, but who cares. These recitals are too long anyway."

The night air was heavy and still. No breeze stirred in the pecan trees standing like sentinels between the church and the street. The Minuet in G, played at an excessively fast tempo, traveled through the oak doors of the Methodist church, as did the ticking of the metronome, which seemed to travel faster than the music. The rapid ticking crossed the street, bounced off the bank building, and returned to the church yard, while Beethoven's minuet seemed to go no further than the two silent pecans. "That metronome is certainly getting on my nerves," Pearl said. "It sounds like it's coming from across the street and inside the church at the same time."

"Sounds like two sets of ticking," said Lefty.

"I've had to live with a metronome all my life," Pearl replied. "I'm about ready for it to stop."

TWELVE

An hour and a half was the scheduled length of the recital, but Miss Fane was determined to end it in sixty-five minutes, and she did. The moment Carlene Hightower finished Beethoven's Minuet in G, Miss Fane, turning off the metronome, leaped to her feet and herded her pupils back on stage for a final bow. She then took Little Teddy by the arm and Demeris by the hand and disappeared out the back door. In the alley behind the church Pearl was sitting in her white, two-door Ford, paid for with her veteran's pension.

Miss Fane was anxious to leave, but Pearl, pretending unconcern, said she was determined for once to take her time.

"What's come over you?" asked Miss Fane. "We've got to get out of here before we're spotted. Why haven't you warmed up this engine?"

"Because I need to be bragged on first," said Pearl, resting her arms on the steering wheel. "You know how to brag, don't you, Mother?"

"Don't you dare brag on her for no reason at all," said Wanda Gay, climbing into the back seat. "We've got to get out of here."

"Bragging is the only way we'll be able to leave on time," said Pearl.

"Oh, all right." Miss Fane spoke through a cramped smile. "I'll play this little game if that's what it takes. I want everybody to know that Pearl is the most reliable member of the family. If I don't call her Reliable, I call her Useful, and if I don't call her Useful, I just call her Pearl, and everybody knows who I'm talking about."

"Well, I guess that will have to do," said Pearl as she started the engine.

When it came to planning the trip from Morehope, Texas, to Canton, Arkansas, there was no question in anybody's mind who would pack the car, select the route, and drive the entire way—Useful Pearl.

"Only a man should be behind the wheel on a trip like this," said Wanda Gay, "that's why Sunday should be going with us."

Miss Fane ignored her.

Sunday had never been much of a driver, but that wasn't the only reason Miss Fane refused to have him on the trip. In her opinion, Sunday had never been much of anything at all but a loafer. She had wanted Wanda Gay to marry a minister because she thought ministers, particularly Methodist ministers, smelled better than other men. But Wanda Gay had disagreed. "In all other ways we see eye to eye, Mother," she had said. "I guess we'll just have to live with this slight difference of opinion."

"You could have had your pick of any man in this town," Miss Fane said as Pearl crept through the alley toward the main street. "But no, you had to pick Sunday Striker. Had you married correctly, we'd have a man behind the wheel right now. You had a choice, Wanda Gay. You just didn't take it."

"No, Mother," Wanda said. "I have never had a choice. Pearl, on the other hand, had several choices."

Of the two sisters, Pearl was considered the more beautiful and personable. As a young girl she was famous for her laughter, for dancing the Charleston with abandon, and for her naturally curly hair. While Wanda Gay and her girlfriends stayed after school to test recipes and practice their sewing, Pearl was often running with her brother and a pack of boys, all honor students and athletes. She would wear their medals and their athletic jackets and stand on the sidelines cheering them on. In spirit they carried her into all their competitions, believing if she were with them they would win, and often they did. "I am only interested in heroes," she would tell Frank, who excelled in basketball and track. Often before an important game or race he would lose his breath and Pearl, always there to support him, would place her hands on his chest and speak to him in a calm voice until he was able to breathe again. She was the sweetheart of all the athletic events. All the young men swarmed around her, eager to be in the presence of her charm, but for those who did not measure up to her expectations Wanda Gay was as close to Pearl as they could get.

"I always had to take Pearl's leftovers," Wanda complained.

"Don't go around saying that," Pearl said. With one hand on the steering wheel she turned to face her sister in the back seat. "You're going to have people believing that Sunday was my boyfriend before he was your husband, and I certainly don't want anybody, even the people I don't like, to entertain the thought that I had so much as once gone out with somebody like Sunday."

"Turn around and watch where you're going before you kill somebody," said Miss Fane while Wanda Gay made a final plea to include Sunday on the trip.

"I am sick of hearing about Sunday," Miss Fane said as the car shot out of the alley and onto the main street. "I realize that it doesn't look right for a carload of women to be going off all by themselves in the middle of the night, but we can't help that. Sunday would just slow us down. You know how he is. Besides, I've brought a man's hat for Pearl to wear behind the wheel. At night no one will know the difference."

Miss Fane wouldn't allow time for a change of clothes. "We'll freshen up when we get there," she said, locking the door with her elbow.

Little Teddy in his ball uniform and Wanda Gay in

her cocktail suit sat in the back seat, with Demeris between them. The tulle skirt of her pink evening gown covered her mother's lap and her cousin Teddy's legs, and the stays of her strapless bodice dug into her tender flesh and made her squirm.

As Pearl sped through a caution light, Miss Fane leaned over the back seat and pointed a finger in her grandson's face. "Mark my word," she said, "for disgracing me with that Little League uniform, you will never have the privilege of performing in another recital."

"That's why I wore it," said Teddy.

"Listen to you," said Miss Fane. "I could slap your face and Pearl's too. You and your mother are just alike. Sometimes I can't tell one from the other. Because of you both, that seemed like the longest recital I ever sat through."

"That seemed like the longest recital *I* ever sat through," said Wanda Gay.

"That seemed like the longest recital I ever sat through too," said Demeris, playing with her skirt.

"Now Pearl, drive a steady speed and don't stop til I tell you to or you'll have the Devil to pay," said Miss Fane.

"Don't stop til you're told to," said Wanda Gay.

"Aunt Pearl," said Demeris, "whatever you do, don't stop til you're told to."

"I'm so tired of being told every little thing from every little person," said Pearl. She adjusted her hat. "I've got a mind left. None of you think so, but I do."

"I remember exactly how I felt then," Pearl would one day write to her grandson. "I remember realizing that we were leaving something behind, and for a moment I wanted to turn around and go back and get it, but what we were leaving behind was nothing that we could go back and get and bring along. It was something intangible and fleeting. A way of life. A way we had with each other. We were abandoning that for a while. For a while everything would be in suspension. Somehow I knew this and I didn't want anything to change and at the same time I realized that I could not fight it any longer. I was, as strange as it must seem to you, comfortable with the way things were before that trip."

THIRTEEN

"I had a sister just like Pearl," Miss Fane once said. "She thought she knew everything, but she didn't. That's why I feel sorry for Wanda Gay. She has to live with what I had to live with and it's not easy. Fortunately for me, Jonsey Marie, my only sister, moved away. Unfortunately for her, she did not live very long after marriage."

Jonsey was five years older than Eugenia. Their father, Eugene Morrison Fane, was a county judge, the owner of an extensive library and the keeper of a mulatto mistress, Cleopatra Smith, who also served the family as housekeeper and occasional cook. Their mother, Perdita Ogletree-Fane, who longed for a concert career, taught piano and entertained Morehope with annual New Year's Eve parties and Fourth of July parties as well as seasonal piano recitals which she performed alone, without her pupils.

"Mother was always jealous because I could play better than she could," Miss Fane would remember. "After a few years she thought I was learning too quickly and refused to teach me anymore, so I had to teach myself and I did it too. I had a natural gift that Mother refused to recognize, and that's why she preferred Jonsey."

Jonsey Marie had no interest in music. She wrote poetry, played chess with her father, and enjoyed reading dictionaries from cover to cover.

"Daddy never loved me like he did Jonsey," Miss Fane frequently reminded Wanda Gay. "That's why he willed our home to the county to house the public library, half of which he had donated himself and all of which Jonsey had read. Daddy never thought I was smart as Sister. But we see where her smartness got her, don't we? Brain tumors don't just happen for no reason at all. Something causes them. That's why I have tried to stop Pearl from making Teddy too smart for his own good. One of these days his head will get so full it'll just pop wide open. Jonsey's did."

"I'm so afraid that will happen to Little Teddy," Wanda Gay would say. "He reads too much, and what he reads is too heavy for a young mind. That's why I only allow Demeris to read ten minutes at a time and never above her grade level. I want her to have a healthy childhood free of mental anguish and petty jealousies, the kind Pearl and Frank inflicted upon me."

When children, Pearl and Frank had refused to accept Wanda Gay as their sister. "You are not one of us," they had constantly reminded her. "We don't know who you are and we don't want to know who you are either." They had amused themselves by playing tricks on their slightly older sister. They caught wasps and turned them loose in her bedroom, picked fleas off stray dogs and put them between Wanda Gay's sheets. They put worms in her shoes and socks, rubbed chili powder on her bar of soap, and chased her with garden snakes, lizards, and frogs.

Wanda Gay had grown up wishing that she had been an only child. She had lived in fear that Frank and Pearl would say or do something mean to her, so she followed her mother around for protection and would scream if her brother and sister came near. Later on she would look back on it all and be thankful that she had grown up so close to her mother. During the last years of her life, she would sit on the porch swing and remind herself that she was the only normal member of the McAlister family. "I spent all my time with Mother," she would say, "and when I got to school, I still wanted to be with her. It is fortunate that I had the forethought to write down almost everything she said, the important things anyway."

Long after Frank's funeral, after Pearl had made her peace with winter, and after the McAlister yard was again filled with St. Augustine grass, Wanda Gay, sitting on the wedding porch, opened a notebook at random and read in her mother's voice. Pearl, listening to the ticking of a distant metronome which measured her sister's recitation, felt like screaming.

"The more you think about what you're doing, the more mistakes you're liable to make. That goes for everything."

"Isn't that good," Wanda Gay said, producing a piece of candy seemingly from thin air and sneaking it into her mouth.

"Just wonderful," Pearl replied. Sitting on the steps with her back turned to her sister, she wondered how many years it had been since the piano in the living room had been opened and the keys dusted.

" 'Potatoes make you fat,' " Wanda Gay read. "If only I had listened to Mother on that account." She turned the page quickly as if to erase a bad memory. "I, like Mother, have lived to see my mistakes staring me in the face," she lamented, "and that's an awful fix to be in."

Carefully turning the pages of her book she found another passage. " 'Someone in our family is a frog that refuses to become a prince.' I should have listened to her on that account too," Wanda Gay said. "Sunday was a frog. It's taken me so long to admit it."

"She was not talking about Sunday in this case," Pearl said. "She was talking about Daddy. Mother thought he looked like a long, thin-faced bullfrog, but had the voice of an angel. She said she married him because he was so ugly on the outside he had to be a jewel inside, and in a way she was right. He just wasn't the kind of jewel Mother could appreciate."

"That doesn't go with my opinion," Wanda Gay said, turning another page. "I've got it recorded in here somewhere where Mother said she married Daddy because he was a handyman."

"Well, he did build this house," Pearl said, "even the columns. And it's still as strong as it was the day he finished it, but that was not *the* reason Mother married him."

Wanda Gay waited for Pearl to say more, but she did not continue. A silence, weighted down by all the years of their lives, surrounded them on that porch where Miss Fane had married Albert and Wanda Gay had married Sunday. Pearl and Frank had refused to marry on the porch because of their fear of becoming too much like everyone else who had been joined there.

After a few minutes of silence, Wanda peered through the window screen, the lace curtains, and into the living room, where a bowl of wilted roses sat on the dusty piano. "Pearl," Wanda Gay whispered, still staring into the house, "do you think Mother can hear us? Do you think she's listening?"

"When Mother was alive she always had her ears open," Pearl said. "I'm sure it's no different now."

Wanda Gay examined the cameo ring on her finger and thought about the overnight trip to Arkansas. "Pearl," she said. "Do you ever think about that trip we took."

"Wanda Gay, do you think I've lost my mind or what?" Pearl stood up to go inside. "How could either of us forget something like that."

"Oh, I'm glad you haven't forgotten," said Wanda Gay. "That means I can ask you another question. Do you think it would have turned out any different if we had taken Sunday along? Sometimes I think it would have."

Pearl did not respond. Somewhere in the house she heard a waltz being played on an out-of-tune piano. Then the ticking of a metronome forced the music into the distance. Searching for the sound, she walked through the dark house without bumping into the furniture. She moved from room to room, pausing in each place long enough to course the ticking. No matter which way she turned it was always behind her, or directly in front of her, never to either side. While Pearl rambled through the dark house, Wanda Gay sat on the front porch and thought about Sunday. "If he had gone along," she kept saying to herself, "Mother would have had one more distraction. And one more distraction might have made things turn out another way."

FOURTEEN

Five miles outside Morehope, Wanda Gay had wanted to turn around in order to say goodbye to Sunday one more time, but Miss Fane would not hear of it. It was the first night Wanda and Sunday had been separated since their marriage, and although they rarely occupied the same bed, Wanda Gay was already missing him.

"How can you miss a beast like that?" Miss Fane hissed. "He's repulsive. Don't deny your feelings. You've stuffed him with potatoes and gravy until he can hardly move, much less swallow another bite, and you've done it on purpose too. Oh, I know a lot you don't think I know, Wanda Gay. I can figure things out just by looking. After one of your starchy meals, all Sunday has the strength to do is roll over and go to sleep. Isn't that right?"

"Sometimes Daddy goes to sleep at the dinner table," said Demeris.

"And who calls the dump truck to get him into bed?" asked Miss Fane. "Demeris, do you do that for your Daddy, sweetheart?"

"No, Mother calls the neighbors," said Demeris.

"Will everybody stop trying to read my mind and figure me out," said Wanda Gay. "I don't like to be figured out, nobody does. For your information, all of you, Sunday has not gone to sleep at the dinner table very often. Not often enough to make an issue of it."

71

"How close is the dinner table to the bed these days?" asked Miss Fane.

"Sometimes Daddy has dinner in bed," said Demeris.

"Just what I thought," said Miss Fane. "Wanda Gay, this separation is exactly what you've been needing. It will do you the world of good. I've been trying to get you separated since the day you married. I always found it necessary to separate myself from Albert."

"You also find it necessary to bathe in the dark," Pearl said, dimming the headlights.

"What does that have to do with Albert?" asked Miss Fane.

"More than you'd like to admit, I'm sure," Pearl replied.

"For your information," said Miss Fane, "water and light together are bad for the complexion, and that's all I intend to say about it. My personal habits will not be discussed on this trip."

"My personal habits will not be discussed on this trip, either," said Wanda Gay.

"I don't have any personal habits to be discussed," said Demeris.

"Don't worry," said Teddy. "I'm sure you'll have some soon."

"I'm hungry," said Demeris. "Is that a personal habit?"

"With Sunday it is," said Pearl.

"Don't remind me of Sunday!" cried Wanda Gay. "There's no one at home to feed him tonight."

"He could last a year without eating," said Pearl. "He's got that much on reserve."

"I'm going to forget you said that, Pearl," said Wanda Gay. "I think that's best. I'm sure Mother will agree."

"Wanda Gay is sensitive about her husband's weight." Miss Fane spoke to Pearl as though Wanda Gay were not present. "It's a subject that cannot be joked about, and he's not getting any smaller either. Pretty soon we'll be able to render him for lard. I've always said, Sunday is sitting on a fortune, and I'm the only one who's smart enough to realize it."

Sunday had not always been fat. He had not always been a spud eater, and he had not always been bald. All that happened after marriage. Not only did Wanda Gay overfeed him, she refused to allow him to do any of the yard work. "Sunday works too hard to bother with the yard," she had informed her friends, "that's why I mow the grass myself."

Before long Miss Fane put a stop to what she called the "unfeminine side of Wanda Gay's yard work." Shortly after Frank had brought home his first wife, the disagreeable Jean, Miss Fane decided it was time to clean up the family's image. She told Wanda Gay that she had been seen pushing a lawn mower for the last time. "If you had a green thumb like I used to have, I'd say it was all right for you to be seen toiling in the yard, but you don't have a green thumb, and it doesn't look good for a woman to be out there mowing like a man. Therefore I have taken it upon myself to hire a man of color to go over and cut your grass and trim your hedges every month. It's obvious to me that Sunday will not lift a finger to do it himself, and the entire town is talking about the way you are forced to be his slave. If only you had listened to me and married a Methodist minister, this town wouldn't be in such an uproar."

Miss Fane had always kept a close eye on Wanda Gay, especially when she started dating Sunday, who was then going by his given name, Jerry. They had been classmates through all twelve grades of public school. Wanda was voted Future Homemaker of America and Jerry was the only student in the history of Morehope High School to fail physical education. "Had it not been for Wanda Gay tutoring him, he would have never graduated," Miss Fane said. "He would have failed everything except shop, the only course he managed to pass on his own. He's not interested in anything, not even sports. That means something's wrong somewhere."

She disapproved of Jerry for many reasons, but the major one had to do with his family. The Strikers lived in a trailer park, and operated a skating rink near the VFW Hall. "If there's anything worse than a trailer park it's a skating rink," Miss Fane had told Wanda Gay. "Low class. That's what I call it. Don't you ever let me catch you at either place."

But Wanda Gay had thought her mother was being unreasonably selfish. "It doesn't matter that his family isn't as prosperous as ours," she had said. "He's all mine. I haven't had to share him with any girl in school, not even Pearl, and that means a lot to me."

"The only reason you get along so well is because you're willing to hide your intelligence to make him feel smart," said Miss Fane. "You never did that for anyone else, but somehow you feel sorry for Jerry Striker, and here he hasn't done a day's worth of work in his life. There's not a muscle on him, not even in his brain, and if you study him close up you'll see that he's covered with a layer of baby fat that will never go away."

Not long after Wanda Gay and Jerry married, he started gaining weight. "I think a little bit of weight is becoming on a man," Wanda Gay had said. "Besides, he won't be all that attractive to other women if he's a little bit heavier."

The more weight Jerry gained, the slower he moved. Miss Fane said he was beginning to look and walk like a balloon filled with water. "All we can do is wait for the explosion," she told the men at the Texaco station who had nicknamed him Sunday. Miss Fane announced her approval by refusing to call her son-in-law Jerry ever again.

"*Sunday* doesn't sound very flattering to me," Wanda Gay said, but in spite of her opinion the nickname stuck and soon she forced herself to accept it as an expression of endearment.

The year after Demeris was born, Sunday developed a head cold that, like his name, was to indelibly mark him for the rest of his life. The cold lingered for weeks and Wanda Gay, attending her husband's sick bed with saintly devotion, prayed for his life to be spared.

"Do what you will," Miss Fane kept saying, "but there's not a prayer in heaven that would save Sunday now. It is my experienced opinion that your husband, Wanda Gay, is going to die, and there's not a thing you or anybody else can do about it. So you might as well relax and allow nature to take its course. Only a miracle could save him now. You see, even a light head cold can be very dangerous for a man who weighs as much as Sunday. He was never healthy to begin with and that was his problem not yours."

"Please do not speak about my husband in the past tense," Wanda had cried. "Not yet anyway."

She kept Sunday lying under an electric blanket two weeks longer than the doctor said was necessary. Gradually he started sitting up in bed for an hour a day. Then, with Wanda's help, he practiced standing. Then he allowed himself to take short walks around the house. Soon he returned to the Texaco station, where he spent most of his days sitting with the water hose and telling customers he was lucky to be alive. Wanda Gay had convinced him that he had almost died, and although the family doctor had assured him that his life had never been in danger, Sunday preferred to believe Wanda Gay, and Wanda Gay preferred to believe Miss Fane: "Sunday almost lost his life, and the next time he gets sick he probably will."

After that Sunday lost almost all his hair and never went outdoors again without a white handkerchief folded in a triangle and tied over his head. The knot divided his second chin. He claimed that the handkerchief protected his head from the cold of the winter and the heat of the summer. "I have a fear of catching another bad cold," he explained. "I also have a fear of the top of my head blistering."

"If Sunday's so afraid of his scalp blistering, why doesn't he wear a hat?" Pearl asked, adjusting the one

Miss Fane had given her to wear on the trip. "Most men who are bald wear hats, not handkerchiefs, on their heads."

"Sunday isn't like other men," Wanda Gay argued.

"At last we agree on something," Miss Fane replied as she examined her cameo ring.

"Mother did not want me to have this heirloom," she said as they sped through the next town. "After Jonsey died she always wished for another heir, just anyone who would treasure this ring besides me. Now I find myself wishing the same thing. Wanda Gay, if I turn this ring over to you, that fat Sunday is liable to have it sold before I'm cold in the ground. Pearl, maybe I should leave it to you."

"No," said Wanda Gay.

"No," said Demeris.

"No," said Pearl. "I don't want it. Only you and Wanda Gay would be seen wearing such an ugly piece of jewelry. I am convinced that it's unlucky and should be buried in some faraway place. Besides, I already have a ring."

She was still wearing her gold wedding band on the third finger of her left hand. Many times Miss Fane had tried to persuade her to move it to another finger, but Pearl had refused. The ring represented Big Teddy. As long as she wore it they were still married, and she intended to wear it to her grave.

FIFTEEN

The first stop was made in the town of Jasper. It was going on midnight and the streets were deserted. "I'm perplexed," Pearl announced as she circled the courthouse square. She was remembering the first time she spent the night in this town. "When I tell you why I'm perplexed you'll say I'm confused, but I'm not confused anymore, I'm just perplexed. Perplexity is different from confusion."

"Perplexed it is, and perplexed you are," said Miss Fane. "Nobody's going to argue with that. You thought you were going to start something, didn't you?"

Pearl parked her Ford in front of the Jasper Hotel and opened the door.

"I didn't tell you to make this stop," Miss Fane said. "This is too close to home. Somebody's liable to see us." She covered her face with her hands as Pearl stepped out of the car.

She stood on the empty sidewalk and stared at a corner window on the third floor of the hotel. "Little Teddy, come here a minute," she said, "I want to show you something."

Little Teddy got out of the car, in spite of his grandmother's disapproval, and stood with his mother.

"That's where Big Teddy and I spent our first night together." Pearl pointed to the window. There wasn't a trace of sadness in her voice and that puzzled her son. "We were madly in love," she said, straining to hold her voice on an even pitch. "I remember it as if it were only yesterday. He had a radio. We turned it on and pretended we were at a grand hotel somewhere. They were playing waltzes that night, all kinds of waltzes, some I haven't heard since then, I'm sure. I've always loved a waltz and your father was a great waltzer, so we pushed back the bed and waltzed all around our little room, which seemed like a palace to both of us. It was spring. There were flowers in the room, and the windows were open. That was the last spring I can clearly remember."

"You always tell me the saddest things," Teddy said.

"That's because I don't have any more sadness left inside me," said Pearl. "I don't have *anything* left inside me. I don't feel sad. I don't feel happy. I don't feel bitter. I don't feel like laughing. Most of the time, I just don't feel."

"Not even when you go to the dentist?" asked her son.

"That kind of pain is different," said Pearl. "It's the kind you never get used to, not really. But there's another kind of pain, the kind you allow yourself to get used to, and that's the most dangerous kind. Pretty soon you don't even notice it. But every now and then it raises its head to let you know it's still there and it's still got you."

"Why don't you just take an aspirin?" asked Teddy.

"If only it could be that easy," said Pearl. "Unfortunately, there's nothing you can take to kill the kind of pain I'm talking about. You've got to make up your mind to ride it out. See where it takes you. That's all you can do."

"Get back in this automobile," shouted Miss Fane.

"Only Mother can make me forget the painful thoughts," Pearl said. "She can make me so angry I can't think about anything else for days, and then I feel better for a little while. When Mother is around it's almost impossible to have problems of your own. At times it's impossible to feel anything except what she wants you to feel."

78

"Get back in this car," Wanda Gay demanded, but Pearl and Teddy ignored her.

"When I married your father," Pearl told her son, "I felt as though the entire world was at my feet. I felt as though there was an entire universe before me, and that I had enough time to do everything I'd ever wanted to do. I don't feel that kind of time surrounding me anymore."

"Maybe you don't want to feel like that now," said Little Teddy.

"I do, and I don't," said Pearl. "I can see it both ways. That's why I'm perplexed."

"Get back in this automobile before you bring further disgrace to our family," shouted Miss Fane. She was standing on the sidewalk and hiding her face with a magazine. Her purple orchid was crushed on her shoulder. "A decent woman doesn't parade around on a sidewalk at this time of night. You're determined to humiliate us, aren't you? You're determined to cause us misery and misfortune and degradation just like your father and just like Frank. Now get back behind the wheel, Pearl, and start driving. I forbid you to make another stop."

"*I* forbid you to make another stop," said Wanda Gay, climbing out of the car.

"Aunt Pearl," shouted Demeris from the back seat. "You better mind." Then she got out too.

Mother, daughter, and granddaughter, all in recital finery, stood one behind the other on the sidewalk that was still holding the heat of the day. "How many times are you going to make me repeat myself?" Miss Fane screamed. Perspiration was pouring down her face.

"Somebody's going to see you," Wanda Gay said. "We're too close to home for you to be behaving this way. It doesn't look right."

Demeris echoed her mother's words.

Pearl pushed back her hat defiantly. "I think I'd like to stay here a little while longer," she said. "I seem to be remembering some things I forgot."

"I think you don't have good sense," said Miss Fane,

taking her daughter by the arm and forcing her back to the car.

Wanda Gay folded her skirt around her legs and squeezed into the back seat. "What would we do without you to keep us in line, Mother?" she said.

"I can think of a lot of things we would do," said Pearl as she backed into the street.

"Then why don't you do some of them?" asked Wanda Gay. "What's stopping you?"

"I don't know," Pearl said. "I sure wish I did."

SIXTEEN

During one period in Pearl's life there had been no one, young or old, telling her what to do—Big Teddy had never given her orders. He had been born in Indiana and stationed during the early part of World War II at Ft. Taylor, only a few miles from Morehope. Pearl fell in love with his voice before she actually met him. At the time she was a telephone operator. She assisted him with a long distance call, and every time he spoke her skin tingled.

"Where did you get a voice like that, and do you have a mind to go along with it?" Pearl had asked her future husband.

"I've got more than a mind," Teddy had answered.

"Well give me the opportunity to judge for myself," Pearl had said. "I never go on the opinion of someone I've never met."

A week later Pearl was sitting in the bus station waiting for Teddy to arrive. Dressed according to her plan for easy recognition, she was wearing a red blouse with massive shoulder pads, a straight black skirt, and a string of pearls around her neck. Her naturally curly hair had been brushed back, away from her face, and was held in place with small combs.

When a soldier, appearing to be lost, stepped off a bus, Pearl's heart pounded. "If you're who I think you are, you better come here and sit down by me," she said, thinking he was most handsome in his uniform.

"I'm just changing buses," the soldier said. "But I have time to buy a pretty girl a Coke."

"You're not Teddy, are you?" Pearl asked without being able to hide her disappointment.

"No," said the soldier. "I'm sorry."

"Somehow I wish you were," said Pearl. "I don't know how anybody could beat your looks."

"Looks aren't everything," he said as they sat down in a booth.

For the first time Pearl noticed that the bus station floor was unlevel and the booth, propped up on one side, slanted in the opposite direction from the floor. "Funny how you notice little things when big things are happening to you, isn't it?" she asked.

"I don't think I know what you mean," he said.

"It's not important," said Pearl. "Just something to say."

Soon the soldier boarded another bus. Pearl did not walk with him to the boarding area. She sat in the booth by herself and waited.

At four o'clock Teddy finally arrived. Pearl took one look at him and said, "Something about you reminds me of my brother, Frank. It must be all that black wavy hair you've got. Frank was in the army too." In comparison to the previous soldier, she was disappointed with Teddy's looks, but that didn't cool her spirit for long.

"What a fine-looking brother you must have," Teddy said in that voice of his.

"Yes, I love Frank very much," said Pearl. "There isn't anything I wouldn't do for him."

Pearl took Teddy's hand and led him to a Plymouth Albert had rebuilt. "This car is accident-proof," she said. "You don't have to be afraid to ride in it." The top had been reinforced with steel and so had the bumpers and fenders. "It was my father's invention," she explained. "You're about to meet him."

"And what about your mother?" Teddy asked.

"I have a father, but I don't have a mother," said Pearl.

"Impossible," said Teddy.

"Not in my case," she replied.

When they arrived at the automobile graveyard, Albert, standing at the entrance to the tin shed where he lived and worked, was holding a hubcap in one hand as though it were a bowl. Gasoline was in the hubcap and so was Albert's free hand. Squinting, more from one eye than the other, he gave Big Teddy a hard look while washing some nuts and bolts in the hubcap. Then he drained off the gasoline and studied the screws, bolts, and washers as though they were tea leaves in the bottom of a cup.

"I believe you're the biggest, tallest, bravest-looking man I've ever seen, next to my son." Albert spoke as though his words were written in the formation of nuts and bolts. "But you cannot marry my daughter."

"We've just met!" Pearl exclaimed. She had never known her father to express an opinion so quickly.

Albert watched his favorite cat circling Big Teddy's legs. His eyes wandered from the cat to Teddy and back to the hubcap in his hands. "I can tell you're thinking about marrying," Albert said, squinting as though looking directly into the sun.

"We haven't talked about that," Pearl said. "Please don't embarrass me any more than you already have."

"There's something too familiar about you, young man," Albert said. "Something too right away familiar about you. That's why I'm going back up to the station with you right now. My daughter's not ready to get married."

Albert sat on the front seat of the Plymouth between Pearl and Teddy. No one spoke on the way back to the station. But after Teddy boarded the bus, Albert warned his daughter not to marry that soldier because he was capable of giving her too much. "He'll make you happy for a little while and then he'll pull you down," he said.

"It's a terrible thing to know too much happiness and then have it ripped away from you."

Disregarding her father's warning, Pearl and Big Teddy continued speaking on the telephone each day. She had great confidence in his military future and was constantly voicing her support. "You have the voice of a winner," she would say. "I have always liked winners. Winners and I get along very well."

Over the telephone they planned their wedding. Pearl had wanted to be married down at the body shop. She had wanted her father to give her away under the tin shed which she had already decorated in her mind. She had wanted Albert to approve of the union, but he refused.

"You approved of Wanda Gay marrying Sunday," Pearl argued.

"Not exactly," said Albert. "She's never seemed like my daughter, so it only seemed like I approved. I didn't really care one way or the other. But with you it's a different matter. You can marry that soldier boy if you want to, but I don't want to see him around here again. I don't approve him, and I don't think Frank would approve him either."

The wedding took place on the army base two weeks after they met. None of Pearl's family was in attendance. "Too far to travel," Miss Fane said. "You haven't known him long enough," Wanda Gay said. "I can't take this marriage very seriously myself," said Frank. He refused to give his sister away and blamed his father for not stopping the wedding.

They were married in the spring of 1942, and Pearl adapted to her new life without a period of adjustment. There were other wives to spend her days with, and in the evenings she and Teddy often went to the movies or the officers' club to dance. Those were the happiest days of her life, and the days against which all the others would soon be compared.

Shortly before the end of the year, Teddy was chosen for a secret mission. A few days before he was scheduled to depart, he withdrew into himself and hardly spoke. He would get up in the middle of the night to drink coffee and smoke cigarettes or play solitaire. And during the day he would often ask Pearl to repeat what she had just said. In the evenings when they went to the officers' club to dance, Pearl felt as if she were holding an empty shell; Teddy was not there. She felt his arms, his face, held his hands and they were cold. His eyes were far away and his voice was different, almost the voice of a stranger. She could not describe the change. It was imperceptible to everyone else, but Pearl noticed it at once: her husband had gone away. She assumed that he was absorbed with the mission assigned to him. He had assured her it was not a dangerous assignment, but the day he said goodbye he told her that he would not return.

"Oh yes, you will return," Pearl said, "I'm convinced of it." She pressed a lock of her hair into Teddy's hand and promised to be with him every step of the way. "You'll come back decorated," she told him. "I know you will."

"Not this time," he said. "Take care of my boy."

Pearl was four months pregnant at the time and Teddy already knew in his heart that she was carrying a son.

"You'll be back," Pearl assured him. "We'll be waiting right here for you."

The day after Teddy left the country, Pearl returned to Morehope to await the birth of her child. She had not seen or spoken to her father since marrying Big Teddy, and was anxious to sit with him in his tin mechanic's shed, and to walk with him through the graveyard. It was mid-January. Snow was on the ground, and ice was bending the trees.

A chromatic scale in two octaves welcomed her back into the house. "Just keep playing until I tell you to stop," Miss Fane said to her student while she took Pearl into the kitchen and closed the door. "The nerve of Louise Johnson, Mary Reynolds, and Lucille Weisenbaker." Miss Fane lashed out at Pearl as if she were at fault. "Those women, all three of them, have called this house to tell me that Albert is sick and must go to the hospital at once. And I told each of them the same thing: 'If Albert is all that sick, why don't *you* take him to the hospital. You've performed every unspeakable act known to man with my husband, what's stopping you from driving him to the doctor?'"

Pearl found the mechanic's shed empty, her father's bed unmade, and the cats unfed. Louise Johnson, one of Albert's regular customers, had already taken him to the hospital where he was lying under an oxygen tent.

"He almost froze to death," Louise said when she saw Pearl. "I tried to get him to come live in my garage apartment but he wouldn't."

Albert died four days after entering the hospital. He died without regaining consciousness, without ever knowing that Pearl had come home. "I just wanted him to know that I was very happy with Teddy," Pearl said to Louise. "I just wanted him to accept what I had done, and not to be angry with me."

"He never wanted you to marry that man because he thought he was going to have a short life," Louise said. "That's what he told me, and he said that Frank had told him. He believed every word that came out of Frank's mouth."

"I hope you took care of him," said Pearl.

"There were many of us," Louise said. "Your father took care of our automobiles, and we tried to take care of him. But he was too proud for his own good. He didn't want help. He wanted to be of help."

A few months later Teddy's prediction came true. Pearl gave birth to a son with black hair and hazel eyes, and a few days later her husband was killed in combat.

When his Purple Heart arrived in the mail Miss Fane wanted to sell it. "This is not something you need to keep," she said. "It will just remind you and go on reminding you of the past."

But Pearl refused to let the golden heart on a purple

ribbon out of her sight. And for a long time she also refused to take off Big Teddy's bathrobe.

"It's against the law for a civilian to wear a Purple Heart," Miss Fane harped. "And here you are parading around with it on your husband's housecoat. You're going to be arrested and locked up. And sometimes I think that's the best place for you."

When Big Teddy's dog tags arrived, Pearl chained them to her right ankle and vowed never to take them off. When the American flag that had covered Big Teddy's coffin was sent home, she kept it folded in a triangle and displayed on her bureau. Occasionally she would fly it in the backyard.

"One of these days she's going to think of a way to wear that flag on her back," said Miss Fane, "and when she does, I'll burn it. So help me I will. I don't care if it *is* my country's flag. Everybody knows how patriotic I am. Everybody knows I try to do the right thing."

That first year after her husband's death Pearl continued to write to him every day. One by one the letters were returned, and each returned letter seemed to send her into a deeper depression than before. After a year of returned letters she decided she had waited long enough. She put away the Purple Heart, the American flag, and the perfumed stationery, as well as her husband's tattered bathrobe.

"Pearl claims she's come back to life again," Miss Fane told her pastor. "But she looks like a walking corpse to me."

She could not accept the fact that she would never see her husband again. Her eyes would cloud over with the slightest mention of his name. At times in the middle of the night she would wake up and go to the front porch to see who was there. No one would be. Sometimes while sitting in church she would feel Big Teddy's presence and get up to look for him. Often she would spend her Sunday afternoons down at the bus station. Dressed in her black skirt, red blouse, and string of pearls, she would sit with

Teddy on her lap and watch the travelers coming and going. And, if not at the bus station, she would be seen wandering through the town with her son in her arms, seldom speaking to anyone along the way.

"If she's not packing that child around, " Miss Fane told Wanda Gay, "she's reading to him out of God knows what book, and that has got to stop before she warps Little Teddy's mind for good. What we've got to do is keep her busy so she doesn't have time to think about herself and all her problems."

Miss Fane and Wanda Gay kept Pearl running. There was always something to be done and Pearl was always the one to do it. At first she welcomed the opportunity to vary her routine. With her son at her side she did the washing, ironing, and housecleaning for both her mother and her sister. She grocery shopped, cooked, and paid the bills. She called the maintenance men and plumbers when they were needed, and often helped them do the work. She was not above climbing onto the roof to help repair a leak or going under the house to replace a pipe. "She's the handiest handyman I've ever known," said Miss Fane. "She's just like her father in that respect; she can fix anything."

"But is she all right, Mother?" Wanda Gay was constantly asking. "You know what I mean. She still doesn't seem like her old self. It gives me an awful feeling to be around her because it seems to me that her thoughts run too deep."

"Listen, Wanda Gay," Miss Fane explained. "Your sister will never be *herself* again. Not after what she's lived through. Pearl has been pulled down by life's tragedies. She's determined to pull me down right along with her, and she's damn near done it. I certainly don't have the kind of pride I used to have. Look at my prize-winning yard. For years my trademark. Gone. Wilted. Dried up. The topsoil washed away and after that gravel was my only answer. I can't even get a bulb to sprout in a flower pot. Furthermore I don't care. I've lost my touch and I do good to keep myself alive."

"Oh no, Mother," cried Wanda Gay. "That means that Pearl's condition is contagious."

"Yes, it is," said Miss Fane. "Pearl's fix is the worst kind of fix to be in, and if we keep reminding her of this, maybe, just maybe, she'll snap out of it. You see, when Big Teddy died in the war, part of Pearl died right along with him. I sometimes wonder which one is better off."

SEVENTEEN

Twelve years after Big Teddy's death, Pearl was beginning to show signs of recovery and that troubled Miss Fane.

"Every once in a while, I start feeling like my old self again," Pearl said, dimming her headlights for the approaching car. "I know that distresses you, Mother, but it's true."

"What distresses me is that you're beginning to lose your usefulness," Miss Fane said. "You're not as reliable as you once were either. This trip has already convinced me of that."

"Fuss, fuss, fuss," said Little Teddy.

"I may be a fuss bucket," said Miss Fane, leaning over the seat and into her grandson's face, "but at least I know when to fuss and when not to fuss. I also know who to fuss at and who not to fuss at."

"Who in this car believes that?" asked Pearl.

"I do," said Wanda Gay.

"I sure don't," said Little Teddy.

"I do too," said Demeris.

"Mother has only fussed at me when it's absolutely necessary," said Wanda Gay. "Demeris, I hope you're listening. I have always tried to follow Mother's good example."

"I've always tried to follow Mother's good example, too," Demeris said to Little Teddy. "Whose example do you follow."

"I'm not sure yet," said Teddy.

"Well, you better be sure," said Demeris. "It's high time."

"I'll be sure when I need to be sure," her cousin replied. "Right now, I'm still thinking about it."

"Thinking, thinking, thinking," said Miss Fane. "Little Teddy is a little thinker if I ever saw one. I don't know how he can come up with so many things to think about."

"I've had a *lot* of help," said Teddy, pushing Demeris's skirt out of his face.

"I bet Little Teddy's thinking about what he's going to be when he becomes a man," said Wanda Gay. "I don't allow Demeris to think about that. She's too young."

"Demeris isn't going to become a man, anyway," said Teddy.

"Pearl, you have taught your son to be a smart aleck," Wanda Gay hissed.

"What *are* you going to be?" asked Demeris.

"I don't know what I'm going to be," said Teddy, "but I do know what I'm going to study."

"What?" asked Miss Fane and Wanda Gay at the same time.

"Abnormal psychology," answered Teddy. "I've been reading about it in the encyclopedias."

"Pearl," exclaimed Wanda Gay. "Did you hear what Little Teddy just said? He used the word *abnormal* in connection with his life. He said he wanted to study abnormality. I heard him, and I would be worried sick if I were you, but of course you're not. I'd throw those books away if it were me, but of course you won't. You'll go on letting him read them even though they're putting all kinds of unclean thoughts in his head."

"Go to sleep, Wanda Gay," Pearl said as a pickup truck carrying a load of lumber flashed its lights and started to pass. Pearl slowed down while the truck returned to the right hand lane.

"Look at that idiot hauling a load of lumber at this hour," Miss Fane said. "You'd think a body would have the sense it takes to stay off the highway in the middle of the night."

"That's what I've been thinking since we started," said Teddy.

"And how long have you been thinking without letting your thoughts be known?" asked Miss Fane.

"A long time," answered her grandson.

"I always think out loud," said Demeris.

"That's your problem," said Teddy. "Not mine."

Suddenly Pearl swerved the car to miss a board that had fallen from the truck. Everyone was thrown first to the left hand side of the car and then the right.

"Warn us next time you decide to do that," shouted Miss Fane. "Do you want to kill us, or what?"

Another board fell from the truck, and Pearl ran over it. A tire exploded and the car lurched to one side.

"What was that explosion?" shouted Miss Fane.

"What was that explosion?" shouted Wanda Gay.

"What was that explosion?" shouted Demeris.

"Everybody knows that sound, so stop pretending." Pearl calmly steered toward the shoulder.

"Oh boy, a flat," said Teddy. "I'm getting tired of sitting here."

Pearl took a flashlight from the glove compartment and got out of the car. Miss Fane followed her. Wanda Gay followed Miss Fane. Demeris followed Wanda Gay. Teddy waited until everyone was examining the tire before he got out and wandered around in the dark.

"I can still see them, but they can't see me," he said. "Just the way I like it."

Miss Fane took the light away from Pearl and stooped to inspect the tire. "I believe it needs to be changed," she said, lifting her skirt off the ground.

"Well of course it needs to be changed," said Pearl. "But I'm not going to be the one to change it because I'm not *that* useful. Besides, I'm wearing my best slacks."

"And you think we're not wearing our best clothes too, I guess," said Wanda Gay. "I spent a lot of money on this cocktail suit." Then she turned to her mother. "Oh, I knew we should have brought Sunday along. Here we are stranded in the middle of nowhere and not a man in sight."

"Somebody's got to change this flat, and it's not going to be me," said Miss Fane.

"Somebody's got to change this flat, and it's not going to be me," said Wanda Gay.

"Somebody's got to change this flat, and it's not going to be me," said Demeris.

"Somebody's got to change this flat, and it's *certainly* not going to be me," said Pearl.

"That's not what you're supposed to say," said Miss Fane, shining the light in Pearl's face.

"I wonder who's going to change it then," said Teddy. He was still standing in the dark.

"Get over here where we can see you," demanded Miss Fane. She was trying to find Teddy with the flashlight, but he was standing behind a tree. "Get over here before you step into a hole or something worse. Now play in the headlights so we'll know where you are."

"I'm not playing," said Teddy, still standing behind the tree.

"Leave him alone, Mother," said Pearl.

"Then what *are* you doing," shouted Miss Fane.

"Standing up," said Teddy.

"Then stand up where we can see you," said his grandmother, waving the flashlight furiously. "Demeris is."

"But I'm not Demeris."

"You see, Mother," said Pearl. "I've raised him to know who he is and who he is not."

Down the highway Wanda Gay spotted a pair of headlights. "Here comes a car," she said. "Let's flag it down." She flashed the headlights on Pearl's Ford.

"I pray to Jesus that whoever is in that car does not entertain thoughts of rape, murder, or robbery," said Miss Fane. "Remember what happened to Mrs. Spurlock when

93

that sex-crazed farm boy broke into their house and tied up her husband and all the children, even the two-year-old?"

"No, what happened?" asked Pearl.

"You already know what happened," said Wanda Gay. "You just want to hear it again because it's abnormal."

"He forced himself on poor Mrs. Spurlock," continued Miss Fane. "While her husband and three children watched, he brutally and uncommonly violated her dignity. And I'm here to testify that nobody in that family has been the same since. There's not one of them I can look in the eye anymore. Imagine having to spend the rest of your life with the memory of such a hideous experience. I pray something like that never happens to us."

"Mother," begged Wanda Gay. "Please don't remind us of tragedy right now. Not when just anything could happen. We have no idea who's going to be in this car."

The automobile came to a slow stop in front of Pearl's Ford. The two pairs of headlights fought for dominance. A man dressed in a wrinkled business suit stepped out of the car. Teddy, standing on the other side of the road, watched the man approach his grandmother, who was holding the flashlight as if it were a pistol.

"If you're not a decent, God-fearing human, get back inside that car and get going," said Miss Fane. "We need help, but we don't need it bad enough to accept it from just anyone."

"I own a horse ranch near here." The man bit into an apple and spoke in a relaxed voice. "If I can't help you I know someone who can."

"Likely story," said Miss Fane. "If you're a rancher, why are you on the road at this time of night?"

"I breed show horses," he said. "But they're not supporting me right now so I travel around selling insurance. You ladies look like you could use some. Here it is almost two in the morning and you're dressed for a wedding."

"A recital!" Miss Fane snapped.

"What's the difference," asked the man.

"Excuse me," said Pearl, stepping into the light.

"Excuse *me*," said the man. "I didn't see you standing there."

"I didn't intend for you to," Pearl replied. "The truth is we *do* need some help. This tire needs to be changed, and we're wearing our best clothes."

"I'll change it for you," the man said without taking his eyes off Pearl. "My name is Charlie."

"My name is Pearl."

"Let me tell you something, Wanda Gay," Miss Fane whispered audibly. "Don't you ever let me catch you giving your name to a total stranger, especially when you're stranded alongside a road."

"I'm wondering," said Pearl, "are you the kind of Charlie who would enjoy being called Charles?"

"Don't talk to him like you've known him all your life." Miss Fane hissed.

"I would," said Charlie, throwing the apple core on the ground. "But nobody ever does."

"Well, I will then," said Pearl.

"You will not," said Miss Fane.

"No," said Wanda Gay.

"No," said Demeris.

"Why not?" came Little Teddy's voice from the dark.

Pearl opened the trunk and Charles removed the spare tire and the jack.

"Pearl," shouted Miss Fane. "You come way over here by this fence and stand with us until that man does what he needs to do. I'll hold the flashlight so you can see to walk."

"This man's name is Charles, Mother," Pearl said.

"Charles *Wakefield*," he said.

"Charles Wakefield," Pearl continued. "He's going to change our flat tire, and I'm going to assist him all I can."

"You will be talked about if you do," said Miss Fane.

"In less than five minutes she knows his full name," whispered Wanda Gay.

"I rather enjoy being talked about, Mother. I enjoy being talked about as much as you enjoy being disagreeable."

"Some family you've got here," said Charles as he assembled the jack.

"You haven't seen anything yet," Pearl said. "Wait til we really get going. There's hardly anything Mother and I haven't said to each other. In a way we don't mean anything by it and in a way we do. It's very hard to explain."

"I guess some people need that sort of thing," said Charles. Teddy walked out of the darkness and sat down near his mother.

"My grandmother does," he said. "If she didn't have somebody to fight with, she wouldn't get out of bed. Uncle Frank said so."

"What's Little Teddy saying?" Miss Fane was clinging to a fence post. "I know he's talking about me."

"In my family," said Charles, stopping to shake hands with Pearl's son, "there are people who enjoy being fussed at and people who enjoy doing the fussing."

"Which one are you?" asked Teddy.

"Neither," said Charles. "I don't fit."

"Neither do I," Teddy replied. "Boy, am I glad."

"Well I can't say I enjoy the way Mother fusses at me all the time." Pearl spoke in a confidential tone that surprised her. "But I've gotten used to it somehow. I've also gotten used to fussing back. Now it's a habit, and I don't know how to break it even though there are times when I'd like to. You see, Mother enjoys our bickering back and forth. Wanda Gay is just as bad, and I guess I am too. If we suddenly stopped fussing at one another, we'd be lost."

"That's the way some families get along," said Charles. "That's the way they show their affection."

"I don't know about that," Pearl said. "I certainly don't hate my mother and sister, but I don't feel affection for them either. I never have. They're simply not my family, not the way Frank is."

"Frank?"

"My brother. We're going to see him."

"He's in jail," said Little Teddy.

"But it's a mistake," Pearl said without being defensive. "He's not a bad person. He's just got a little too much of Daddy in him."

"And where is Daddy tonight?" Charles asked, removing the wheel.

"Resting, I hope," Pearl said. "He certainly deserves to."

"He died the year I was born," explained Teddy.

"Everyone in Morehope thinks Mother aggravated him to death," Pearl said, "and she probably did. He was a mechanic and enjoyed a rather devoted clientele of lady friends. Daddy was not handsome, if anything he was rather ugly, but there was something about him that women loved, especially Louise Johnson. She cried so much at his funeral she had to leave."

"He had eight cats when he died," Teddy said, "and Louise took them all home with her. She's still got three of them."

"That's right." Pearl, eager to amuse, jumped back into the conversation. "But his favorite one went to sleep under the hood of Mary Reynold's car, and when Daddy tested the engine the cat was sliced to pieces. Mother says that he was never the same after that. She says he grieved over that cat until the day he died. I say he hated what happened, of course, but he sure didn't grieve himself down and out over it. It was Mother who finally got him down. He didn't enjoy contention, so he moved into his mechanic's shop. It was cold and drafty and he wouldn't live anywhere else, so eventually he got sick and died."

"What are you talking about, Pearl," Miss Fane shouted, as Charles replaced the flat tire with the spare. "Speak up, so I'll know what's going on."

"Mother has always chosen the most docile people

to pick on," Pearl said. "For a while she thought I was one of them, but I've turned out to be a surprise to her. Sometimes I can't believe some of the things that come out of my mouth. Most of the time there's no emotion behind what I'm saying. Most of the time I don't even listen to myself. But when I do, I'm shocked. I'm shocked that I say what I say, and shocked that Mother actually needs me to say these horrible things to her. In a way I give her what she needs. But often at my own expense."

"At your expense or your son's expense?" asked Charles.

"Both," answered Little Teddy. "I think we should move away. I hate Morehope. The only thing I like about Morehope is Little League, and Little League is everywhere, isn't it?"

"Even in Longview," Charles said.

While he positioned the spare tire, he told Pearl that he had lived in Longview all his life, and that he had been married twice. "Two sons by my second wife," he said. "I'm raising them myself, but I'm too old now to think about marriage again. I'm set in my ways and can't change."

"Maybe you don't have any ways that need changing," said Pearl, not realizing she was being flirtatious.

"I have six show horses," Charles said, abruptly changing the subject. "Their stables are better-looking than my house. One of these days the horses will support me and then I'll do some work on *my* place."

"All you need is a push," said Pearl. Already she was interested in this man. She liked his looks, and his manners, and the tone of his voice. She liked his clean fingernails and his black hair combed back on the sides.

"My husband was killed in the war," she said, immediately regretting having volunteered the information. "Well, actually," she added, "I don't intend to marry again, either. I've got my mother and son to look after. That's all I need."

"I suppose you know what's best for them," said Charles. "But do you know what's best for you?"

Pearl was silenced by the question.

"Be sure you get the wheel on tight!" shouted Miss Fane. "We sure don't want it to come off on the road. Tighten all the nuts a little bit at a time, not one all the way and then the others. If you don't *listen* to me we'll have a wobbly wheel."

"*Listening* isn't *doing*," Charles said. "She's always like this. Right?"

"Right," said Teddy. "What she has is an inferiority complex, but at first you might think it's just the opposite. You should try living with her."

"No thanks," said Charles.

After he had finished changing the flat, he wiped his hands on the grass. Pearl returned the jack to the trunk of the car, and Miss Fane ventured forward to inspect the tire. "This better be on tight," she told Wanda Gay. "If it's not, he'll have to do it over."

"He'll have to do it over if it's loose," said Demeris.

"You're not supposed to jump ahead," said Wanda Gay, obviously irritated. "Let me speak before you, please."

Miss Fane kicked the tire to test it while Pearl said goodbye to Charles. Leaning on the open door of his Chevrolet while he sat behind the wheel, she wondered what his children were like, but she would not allow herself to inquire. "What are you doing out on the highway this time of night?" she asked instead.

"I've been on the road all day," said Charles, turning on the car radio, "so I stopped over at this dance hall called The Torch."

"Dancing," said Pearl. "It's been years. I don't even know if I could anymore. My husband and I used to go dancing all the time."

"Goodnight Irene" was on the radio. Charles turned the volume up.

"That's a waltz, isn't it?" asked Pearl. "Funny, I never realized that 'Goodnight Irene' was a waltz until now. I just love a waltz better than anything. Big-Teddy-who-died-in-the-war was the best waltzer in the world."

"I'm not bad myself." Charles got out of the car and took Pearl in his arms. As they waltzed into the bright light between their cars, Pearl could smell apple on his breath and the lingering scent of aftershave.

"You *do* know how to waltz," she said, giving herself to the moment. "You're almost as good as Teddy."

"We'll have no more of this," said Miss Fane honking the horn. "This isn't a nightclub. For God's sake, somebody give the man a dollar for his trouble and let's get going."

Little Teddy, standing on the driver's side of the car, watched his mother. He had never seen her dancing before. In fact, he had never known her to be so talkative either. "I think Mother is having a good time," he said.

"Nonsense," said Miss Fane. "Here. Take this dollar bill and give it to the man and tell him to turn your mother loose."

"He wouldn't take it," said Teddy, refusing the money.

"Well then, he can't say I didn't offer to pay him for his trouble," said Miss Fane, returning the dollar to her purse.

"No he can't, Mother," replied Wanda Gay. "I bear witness to that."

Charles waltzed Pearl down the center stripe of the highway and into the dark. The car horn now seemed to fade into the distance as Pearl, lost in time, imagined she was in Teddy's arms again. "The Officers' club," she whispered into Charles' ear. "How I love the Officers' club. I want to come here every night."

She recalled the first and last New Year's Eve she had spent with her husband. Deliriously happy, she had felt that life would go on forever and would continue, in spite of the war, to be wonderful. That had been a joyous New Year's celebration. The Officers' club had been decorated with paper lanterns but in Pearl's memory they were crystal chandeliers. And the champagne, although far from the finest, was like liquid gold, and the dress, that Ginger Rogers dress, had always been her favorite.

"Do you like this dress?" Pearl whispered into Charles's ear. "I chose it with you in mind."

"But you're not wearing a dress," Charles said, at once realizing he had said the wrong thing.

Startled back to reality, Pearl tightened her grip on Charles's hand and shoulder. Her entire body became rigid in his arms. No longer did her feet follow his in an unbroken rhythm. Instead, he seemed to drag her along for a few steps, and then the music stopped.

"Oh, make it start up again," said Pearl.

"This is a good station," said Charles. "They'll play something else very soon." But the next song was not a waltz, and Pearl, embarrassed that she had gotten carried away, tried to apologize.

"I'm sorry," she said. "I don't know what I could have been thinking."

"Something about a dress," Charles reminded her. "Ginger Rogers's dress."

"Oh yes," said Pearl. "Sometimes I think if I could only find that dress, the entire world would be a better place again. I know that sounds silly."

"Not at all," Charles replied. Holding her face in his hands, he brought his lips close to hers.

"Not now," Pearl said. "Big Teddy was the last man who kissed me, and I don't want that to change."

Without uttering another word, Pearl ran back to her car, the military tags on her ankles jangling in the dark.

Charles waited until she started the engine and drove off. For a long time he sat there thinking about what had just happened. "Pearl," he kept saying over and over. He considered turning around and following her, but instead he continued on his way, driving in the opposite direction.

EIGHTEEN

"Your grandmother Perdita was famous for her fancy dresses, her party invitations, her unconventional behavior, and her lively dancing," said Miss Winnie Barlow, the oldest citizen of Morehope and the only resident of the local retirement home who still had her right mind. At the age of 103, Miss Winnie could remember attending Perdita's parties and sitting with her during her long depression after the death of Jonsey. Standing over Frank's Brazilian coffin, Miss Winnie told Pearl that Perdita had been the *artistic type*. "She was what we called *spirited* back then," she said, holding Pearl's arm for support. "You should have seen her on the dance floor. There was no one like her. There was no one in this town who knew how to appreciate someone like Perdita. You see, she had the courage to do exactly what she wanted to do. In the middle of a dinner party she once took her plate and sat behind a couch because she suddenly felt the need to be alone. That's the way she was, and she was vain too. If she thought she looked tired, she would drape a scarf over her head so no one could see her. If she couldn't make her hair do what she wanted it to do, out would come the scarf and over her head it would go. You could never predict Perdita. She was like velvet. You had to stroke her to know which way the nap was running. All at once she would take the notion to change the subject, change her dress, put on a different hat, get up and walk out without a goodbye and not come back to the party. Maybe that's the way she was reared, we didn't know. We didn't know very much about her except that her father taught school and her mother was a poetess greatly admired. The Ogletrees came from Tyler where the roses grow, and Morehope didn't suit Perdita a bit. Neither, I might add, did her marriage to Judge Fane."

Perdita had musical aspirations which went unfulfilled, but that, Miss Winnie was convinced, was only part of what made her so unhappy and restless. "Her mental health deteriorated beyond repair when she realized what was going on under her very own roof," Miss Winnie explained. "I am talking about that Cleopatra Smith. This entire town knew, long before Perdita, that the judge had taken Cleopatra into his heart."

On realizing her husband's infidelity, Perdita moved him into his own bedroom, which he rarely used, preferring instead to occupy the attic with Cleo, who had beautiful legs and delicate ankles. Late into the night Perdita would sit at the keyboard and play Brahms or Beethoven to drown out the sounds of the squeaking bed, which would follow her from room to room into the far corners of the house. Even in the afternoons when Cleopatra was cleaning or darning and the judge was in his office Perdita would hear the bed squeaking and the window panes vibrating. "Am I to be driven mad by the sounds of love-making?" she had asked her younger daughter. "Your father is concentrating on two things and two things only, how to drive me out of my mind or out of this house and he has almost done both. As you see, I have already removed my wedding band, and I have a good mind to turn this cameo over to Jonsey Marie along with the entire household. She's old enough to run it properly and I can depend on her to get you to school on time."

Perdita had no intention of relinquishing her mother's ring, and Jonsey had no intention of remaining at home any longer than necessary. She married a lawyer and moved away from Morehope. She set up a home of her own, and was planning a family when tragedy struck.

"Brain tumors don't just happen," Perdita cried. "Something causes them. Something brings them on. Jonsey was upset over her father's behavior. She was worried about me. She was distressed. The pressure on her brain was more than she could endure."

After Jonsey's death Perdita took to her bed to read tragedies, eat chocolate, and ring the bell for Cleo to wait on her. Up and down the stairs Cleo ran, carrying magazines, and coffee, and fresh bedsheets. Perdita insisted on having her sheets changed twice a day. She insisted on five small meals instead of three large ones. She insisted on fresh flowers brought in daily and window curtains changed several times a week. Back and forth along the steep stairs Cleo traveled, carrying miniature meals, and beverages: coffee at 8:00 a.m. followed by midmorning chocolate, afternoon tea, and glasses of ice water. "That woman can ask for more glasses of water than anyone I've ever worked for," Cleo told the judge. "And what she wants she wants right now, no waiting."

Spending so much time on the stairs caused Cleo's feet to swell and ache. For support she wrapped her ankles with rags but the judge protested. "Your ankles are delicious," he told her, "I don't want them covered up."

In her bedroom Perdita, mourning her daughter's death, overheard the judge extolling the beauty of Cleopatra Smith's ankles and legs. "And why aren't you at the keyboard," she said to Eugenia. "If you were playing the piano your father's harsh words would not reach my ears."

Eugenia, always ready to win her mother's approval, spent many hours a day at the keyboard. "Too fast," Perdita would shout down the stairs. "Follow the designated dynamical markings and tempos." For a few bars she would remain silent and then her nerves would flare again. "Too slow," she would shout to her only living daughter. "Why are you and your father out to torture me to death."

Eugenia played according to her mother's desire. If Perdita called for a slower tempo, Eugenia played with a slower tempo. If she screamed for speed, Eugenia's fingers would race across the keyboard. At times Perdita would appear at the top of the stairs, a black scarf draped over her head, and tap out the tempo until Eugenia's fingers moved with the cadence her mother required in order to fall asleep, or daydream, or clear her mind long enough to write anonymous letters and invitations to her friends.

"I still have two of your grandmother's invitations right here," Miss Winnie told Pearl as the mourners crowded around Frank's foreign coffin. From a canvas sewing bag with clacking wooden handles, the retired schoolteacher brought forth an invitation composed by Perdita and written by Eugenia.

On Thursday afternoon at 3:00 a surprise tea party will be held in honor of Mrs. Perdita Ogletree-Fane, who lives in deepest mourning over the death of her beloved daughter. Friends of Mrs. Ogletree-Fane are requested to gather in the parlor until everyone has arrived, at which time they may proceed up the stairs to the bedchamber where the surprise party will be held. Please bring small tokens of love for our dear Perdita, who has been confined to bed since her tragic loss.

A friend of Mrs. Perdita Ogletree-Fane

"If Perdita wasn't planning another surprise for herself, she was forcing your mother to play the piano," Miss Winnie remembered. "I often sat in her sickroom trying to cheer her up, but Perdita just couldn't be cheered. Nothing pleased her. She would sit in bed and shout to Eugenia, 'If you stop playing I surely will die.' Then a few minutes later she would say, 'If you do not follow the correct tempo and dynamics I will throw myself down the stairs from sheer frustration. You are driving me out

105

of my mind with your irregular cadences. I must have laughter. Where are the happy voices? Where are my cheerful friends?'"

"Nobody could keep up with Perdita," Miss Winnie said, producing the second of the two invitations she had kept. "Here is another example of your grandmother's mind at work." She gave the invitation to Pearl.

Mrs. Perdita Ogletree-Fane, who has not been well since the loss of her beloved daughter, Jonsey Marie, is in deepest need of convivial distraction and would appreciate surprise visits from her dearest friends. Mrs. Ogletree-Fane resides in her bedchamber and may be visited each afternoon between the hours of two and four. Gifts of love may be bestowed on our dear Perdita, whose health continues to decline.
A Friend of Mrs. Perdita Ogletree-Fane

"Poor mother," Pearl said after reading the invitation. "No wonder she turned out to be a raving maniac."

"Perdita was too sensitive for her own good," Miss Winnie replied. "Everything pulled her down. Cleopatra Smith was the starting of it, but losing that daughter finished her off. After Jonsey Marie died, Perdita was never the same again, certainly not at her last party. She got all dressed up one last time and I almost didn't recognize her. Nobody did. She had changed somehow. She had changed in the face somehow. I guess her mind had already crossed over and nobody realized it or else we just didn't want to admit that Perdita was no longer with us."

NINETEEN

While everyone slept, Pearl exceeded the speed limit to make up for lost time. Throughout her life she would think back to this moment and wish that she and Teddy had gotten into Charles's car and left the rest of the family stranded by the side of the road. As an old woman sitting on the wedding porch and watching the world pass at an interminably slow speed, she would often find herself wondering what would have happened if she had allowed Charles to kiss her, or if she had turned the trip over to Wanda Gay. Would that have changed anything that happened later on that day?

The most relaxing part of the trip she would remember were the few minutes after she said goodbye to Charles. While everyone slept she drove in silence. On the back seat Wanda Gay leaned against the door and Demeris leaned against Wanda Gay. Up front Teddy slept with his head resting on Pearl's shoulder, and next to him Miss Fane slept with a rayon scarf draped over her head and face.

"A person does not present a pleasing picture while sleeping," she had always said. "That's why I never allow anyone into my bedroom before I wake up. That's why the door is always locked."

The silence in the car was sacred to Pearl. "If Mother knew how much better we like her when she's sleeping," she said when her son woke up, "she'd never go to sleep again."

Teddy sat up and stared at the highway. "Did you like that man?" he asked.

"I don't know," said Pearl. "Are there any apples in that sack of fruit Mother brought?"

"Don't change the subject so quickly please," said Teddy. "If you don't know whether you liked him or not, why did you tell him all that stuff about us?" He handed Pearl a soft apple and she bit into it as though starving.

"I was nervous," she said. The sweet aroma of the apple almost made her sick. She threw it out the window.

"Why were you nervous?"

"Because . . . well, I guess I did like him. I guess I wanted to impress him."

"Then why don't you just say so? What's wrong with that?"

"Did *you* like him?"

"Yes, I did. I liked him a lot. He was better than that pharmacist with the thin moustache. I hated him. His hands were always damp. I didn't like that schoolteacher who liked you either. He was too serious, and that preacher was too gloomy. Besides, when he brought you those flowers that time, he felt ridiculous."

"How do you know how he felt?"

"I could feel him feeling," said Teddy. "Couldn't you? He was ludicrous."

"Where did you learn that word?" asked Pearl.

"I liked Charles," replied Teddy. "I'd like to ride his horses."

"But he was nothing like your father," Pearl said.

"Sometimes I get tired of hearing about him," said Teddy. "I just wish he would go away. Nobody could be all that good."

"We're crossing the state line," said Pearl, relieved to have an excuse to change the subject. "We're in Arkansas now."

It was 4:00 a.m. To keep from awakening everyone

Pearl came to a very slow stop behind an all-night service station. She parked in the shadows and whispered to her son to get out of the car without making a sound. They rolled the flat tire into the station and asked to have it repaired. Then they crossed the highway to a cafe and took a booth near a window.

"If we're lucky," Pearl told Teddy, "they won't wake up any time soon. And we can have this time to ourselves. Won't that be nice?"

"Do you think Charles drinks coffee?" Teddy asked.

Pearl ignored her son's question.

"I bet he does," Teddy said. "What do you think?"

Pearl did not answer.

"I'm going to order a cup of coffee," said Teddy.

Pearl smoked and read the menu.

"Do you think Charles's horses drink coffee?" Teddy asked.

Again Pearl ignored his question.

"Sometimes I think you go out of your way to irritate me, Mother," Teddy said. "One of these days, I'd like for you to answer my important questions."

Pearl was silent. She looked up from the menu and into her son's eyes. Sometimes she wondered who he was and where he had come from. "Whose boy are you anyway," she wanted to say. "How did you happen?"

"Do you think," asked Teddy, "that I will ever get to ride a horse?"

"Yes!" Pearl said, almost raising her voice in exasperation. "For God's sake, Teddy, when we find a horse that's gentle enough, you can ride it. Now please. What do you want to eat?"

"Just coffee, please."

Pearl ordered breakfast for both of them, and tried to ignore the stares coming to her from all corners of the cafe. She was the only woman present, except the waitress.

"All these men are staring at you, Mother," Teddy said.

"That always happens," Pearl said. "That's why we

seldom go outside Morehope. I can't stand it when people stare."

"But they're not bad stares," said her son.

"All stares are bad stares," said Pearl. "Staring is rude."

"Even if you like what you're staring at?" asked her son.

"Eat your breakfast," she said. "Here, drink my coffee. Do something besides talk."

"Well, I stare at everybody," said Teddy. "So that makes me rude. But I can't help it. If we went more places maybe I wouldn't stare so much."

"Are you enjoying this trip?" asked his mother.

"It could be better," Teddy said. "If Uncle Frank were with us, we'd be having more fun. And if Shirley were here, we'd really be having a lot of fun."

"Will you ever forget Shirley?" Pearl asked.

"She was the best," Teddy said. "Of all of Uncle Frank's wives, Shirley was the most fun."

Throughout his life, Teddy would live with a vivid image of Frank's second wife, third, if counting the common-law Gloria. Frank brought Shirley home from the Gulf Coast where he had been working at the time, and Miss Fane had demanded to see the marriage license before allowing them inside the house. She inspected the license with a magnifying glass to spot any signs of forgery and finally, against her wishes, she declared the document acceptable. "You can only stay for the weekend," she said. "You can use Albert's old room. That way you will have your private entrance and won't need to traipse through my house."

Shirley wore the same clothes every day: dark stockings with seams, white heels, and a tight, black skirt with a kick pleat. She was a full-figured woman whose breasts were so large she could barely button her red bandana blouse.

"There's nothing more vulgar than a blouse stretched

to its limits," Miss Fane had said. "I can see the woman's flesh between the buttons."

"I liked her because she knew how to play." Teddy rested his legs on the seat in front of him. "She was always ready to have a good time, especially in the sand." Down on her hands and knees in her seamed stockings, straight skirt, and tight red blouse she had helped him build a sand castle that he would never forget. Frank had taken a snapshot of his wife and nephew kneeling on the sand next to their creation. Both were covered with dirt and water, and Shirley's platinum hair was hanging perfectly straight, like silk threads.

"I have never trusted a woman who didn't have some body in her hair," Miss Fane had said, when she saw the photograph. "That tramp looks right at home down there in the dirt. That's where she belongs."

"Who do you think stole that picture of me and Shirley playing in the sand?" Teddy asked his mother. The diner was filling up with truck drivers.

"Mother," Pearl said. "Who did you think?"

"I thought so," said Teddy. "I sure wish I had it back. I liked Shirley."

"And Marsha? What about her?"

"Well, I liked her all right, but I wasn't crazy about her, especially after she shot Uncle Frank in the leg. Basically Marsha is too crazy to be much fun. She thinks she was born on Mars and that one day she'll find a way of going back."

"I wish it would be soon," Pearl said. "Frank's in trouble and she's probably got a lot to do with it."

"I think people should leave him alone," said Teddy. "He should be able to have as many wives as he wants as long as they aren't dangerous."

"All of Frank's wives have been dangerous." Pearl glanced up to see all eyes turning her way. "We've got to hurry," she said. "All these men are staring again."

"I don't understand what's wrong with that," Teddy said. "Didn't my father stare at you too?"

"Your father was a decent man," Pearl answered. "He may have been the last decent man on earth for all I know."

Without finishing breakfast, Pearl took her son by the hand and hurried across the highway. "I couldn't stand it in there another minute," she said once they reached the service station. "Everyone was staring with intentions."

"So what?" said her son.

After the tire was repaired, Pearl drove into the bright lights of the station and asked the attendant to fill the tank. Miss Fane woke up and, without removing her sleeping scarf, told Pearl to ask for full service. "Be sure that man cleans off the windshield before you drive away," she said. "Whether it needs it or not that's his job and he's supposed to do it. I believe in getting my money's worth, even when I'm not paying."

In the backseat Wanda Gay and Demeris sat up quickly.

"Go back to sleep, all of you," Pearl said. "I don't believe in waking up until it's absolutely necessary."

TWENTY

On a day in the future, after everything had been said and done, Pearl, basking in the few moments of silence she had managed to stumble into, sat on the porch swing and thought of Frank. He had been buried that morning and many of his friends and relatives had returned to the McAlister house with plates of food and words of respect. Inside, everyone seemed to be talking at once, but on the porch, Pearl had drifted away. She was not aware of the comings and goings of mourners, of the scraps of conversations wafting through the windows and lingering on the front yard where St. Augustine grass was waging a battle with the gravel.

Earlier in the day Miss Winnie, during her brief appearance at the funeral home, reminded everyone that she had not only taught Pearl, Frank, and Wanda Gay, but Eugenia Fane as well.

"Your mother could not grasp the difference between dependent and independent clauses," Miss Winnie told Pearl. They stood to one side of the mourners, chatting, their faces pressed close together. "Some things were lost on Eugenia. It took us three years to repair the damage her sister Jonsey Marie had caused. Nowadays if such a thing were to happen, it would make all the newspapers, but then no one thought much of it."

Miss Winnie said that Eugenia was sent to school in a state of confusion, which Judge Fane had found amusing and Perdita, too busy with her recitals and parties, her pretty dresses and home decorations, had almost totally disregarded.

"Let young Miss Winnie handle the problem," Perdita had said. "She's a professional. That's why we send our children to school."

Eugenia Fane had arrived in Miss Winnie's class thinking that circles were squares and squares were triangles. Jonsey had taught her that green was blue, and red was yellow, and right was left. "When she came to class that first day, none of us realized how serious the problem really was," Miss Winnie said. "It took us several weeks to determine that she was not pretending but was totally confused, thanks to Jonsey Marie, who was brilliant, yes, but could not be depended on to tell the truth. She had taught Eugenia and taught her thoroughly that feet were inches and inches were yards, and yards were feet."

"I never knew that," said Pearl. "No wonder Mother always said a square of yarn, instead of a ball of yarn. No wonder she hated her sister so much."

"Not only her sister," Miss Winnie said, "her mother as well. Eugenia did everything in her power to get Perdita's attention. But nobody except Jonsey could get Perdita to look around with admiration. Jonsey would read poetry to Perdita. She would read the Psalms to Perdita. She would deliver Shakespeare sonnets by memory to Perdita. And she did have the most melodious voice in the world. The most soothing, the most tranquil voice anybody had ever heard. Perdita called her The Angel. Eugenia, on the other hand, was just the opposite. She would bang around on the piano the day long if she felt like it. You could hear her all over town. The same old pieces over and over. She played them every tempo in the book and still she couldn't satisfy Perdita."

While Wanda Gay and Demeris had argued over the placement of the family wreath, and young Teddy sat in the lobby with his fiancée, Miss Winnie had tried to set Pearl straight on the story of her parents' marriage.

114

"Judge Fane had been totally against the courtship," Miss Winnie remembered. She pronounced what she said were the judge's exact words to his unmarried daughter: "That boy comes from a questionable background of carpenters and traveling cabinet makers. They can build houses, but they don't know how to live in them. They don't know how to stay put. Why can't you follow your sister's example and marry a lawyer? If not a lawyer or a doctor, someone who has a formal education or the desire to receive one."

Miss Winnie said that for years Eugenia had held Albert at arm's length. During that time he proposed over and over and each time she refused to answer yes or no. Finally he asked her, "What will it take for you to become my wife?" Eugenia answered with what she believed to be an impossible request.

"It would take a big house," she had said. "I would want you to build me a great big house that looks exactly like me and I would want you to build the porch first so I'll have some place to sit while the rest of the house is going up."

Albert designed the house in the Greek revival style because he thought his future wife was beautiful enough to be a goddess. With bank loans and the help of his brothers the house was built within a year and during that time Eugenia Fane sat on the porch with her girlfriends and supervised the builders. She told them exactly what to do, and exactly what not to do and they pretended to follow her instructions all the way. When the house was completed she walked across the street to study it, her jealous bridesmaids following in her steps. She glanced at the house and without hesitation—for she had already decided her response—she said: I don't like it. It won't do. It's not me."

Miss Winnie was convinced that Eugenia Fane never intended to marry Albert or anyone else. She said that Eugenia was the ringleader of a pack of girls all of whom were under her sway. She made them promise that they

115

would never marry and never take a man into their arms, and in English class they wrote papers extolling the virtues of the independent woman. "Eugenia had them believing that no man could be trusted," Miss Winnie said. "She told them they were supposed to be virgins for the rest of their lives and then Albert came along and all but Eugenia lost their wits over him. When she realized that she was losing control over her group she decided she would court Albert to the envy of her friends. 'None of you can marry,' she told them 'until I have made my decision and walked down the aisle.' Many times Albert knelt before her and many times she led him on with half promises. When she outright rejected the house, Judge Fane stepped in. 'I don't like him any better than before,' he said, 'but at this point you've gone too far to change your mind.' By then all the ladies-in-waiting were tired of waiting. Many of them were engaged and setting their own wedding dates regardless of Eugenia's demands, so she decided to act fast in order to be the first to wed."

The ceremony took place on the far end of the porch which wrapped around one side of the house. As soon as the bride and groom moved in, Eugenia resigned from her job as church organist and began teaching piano in her living room. Six days a week from eight in the morning until seven in the evening she taught young people as well as a few adults how to play Bach, Brahms, and Beethoven, while Albert retreated further and further into the house for his own peace of mind.

"Finally," Miss Winnie said, "your father gave up working with his brothers and followed his passion, automobile mechanics and women in need of love. He stopped attending church, and stopped singing, and eventually he moved out. None of us knew what took him so long. 'Albert may have built this house,' Eugenia went around saying. 'But I'm the one who's paying for it. We can't live on Albert's so-called profession. He's too much of a perfectionist. He repairs every little thing, and after he's repaired a car once it's like brand new. I keep telling him that he must not be so thorough, else he'll work himself out of a job.' "

After Frank's funeral, when everyone returned to the McAlister house, Pearl, disregarding the scraps of conversation that could be heard on the porch, tried to remember the exact year her father had moved to the body shop. "I believe I was in Miss Winnie's sophomore class when Daddy moved out," she said to her son when he joined her on the swing. Rebecca, his future wife, a Colorado blond with clear skin and blue eyes, remained inside. "Mother," he said, "I have something to tell you. Rebecca and I are going to be married this summer."

"But there's not one thing interesting, unusual, or exciting about her," said Pearl. "I have never seen that girl laugh, cry, or display the slightest trace of emotion of any kind. Surely you can do better than that."

"And what else is wrong with her?" asked Teddy.

"Her personality," Pearl answered. "She hasn't got one. She doesn't have a body either. Why do girls want to be so skinny nowadays?"

"Mother," Teddy said. "We want to be married right here on this porch."

"Oh no you don't!" Pearl stood up to lecture her son. "Anywhere but here. Even if I liked her I wouldn't allow you to marry her on this porch. I'm convinced that she's a bad choice, and that you'll have a terrible life together, and I am also convinced that it will be even worse if you marry on this porch. If I thought you had the mind to disobey me on this issue, I'd burn this entire house to the ground."

TWENTY-ONE

At 8:30 Frank's family arrived in Canton, a town of five thousand, with a consolidated high school, six churches, and a county seat. "Take me to the first motel you come to," Miss Fane said, slipping a sweet into her mouth. "I've got to freshen up in order to make a good impression. Right now, I'm hot, tired, and sticky and that's an awful fix to be in. On top of everything else I've got to have my insulin fast. If I don't take my shot soon, I'm liable to lose control of myself, and I pray no one in this car is wishing for that. Oh Lord, if you let me live through this day, I'll claim a miracle."

It was the second Saturday in May, opening day for the Tri-State Band Festival. Fifty-eight high schools were competing in three categories: marching, concert-playing, and solo and ensemble for musicians and twirlers. Students were squeezed into every available living space. Not a room could be found. Finally, Pearl gave up searching for a vacancy and parked in front of the county jail, a three-story building of white stone sitting on an expansive lawn. The building looked more like a courthouse or a hotel, and in fact had once been a private residence. Six small cells were located on the third floor. The second-floor offices were approached by a double staircase, each section of which made a gentle curve from the lawn and met on a small porch. In the ground-level residence lived the jailer, Sam Sticks, and his wife, who was called Silly because she was.

When Frank's family arrived, Silly, who took measurements for custom-made foundation garments, was moving her husband's geranium to the sunny side of the high porch between the two staircases. The geranium, which Silly called "Sam's pet," grew in a clay pot and had its own chair to sit on.

"If you want this thing to go on living, you better come water it right now," Silly shouted to her husband, who was sitting in his office. Then she hung a "Welcome" sign above the entrance to the jail. During Tri-State Band Festivals and special holidays the sign was always brought out. "Even the jailbirds welcome you to this town," Silly shouted to the twirlers on the lawn. But they weren't listening. "Everybody's got too much to do to pay attention to anybody else," she said to the geranium. Silly was somewhere in her late fifties, and everything about her was short except her temper. She showed gums when she smiled and two of her front teeth were edged in gold.

"Stop acting silly," Miss Fane shouted to Demeris.

"Who called my name?" asked Silly. She put on a green visor to shade her eyes.

Demeris, happy to be out of the car, was skipping down the sidewalk toward three baton twirlers who were rehearsing a new ending to the routine they were scheduled to perform for the judges that afternoon. When she had the attention of the twirlers, she did a backbend in her formal and couldn't get up without first lying down.

"Maybe we should try something acrobatic," said Linda Margaret, the leader, who was famous for her aerials.

"You mean like that little girl in the evening gown," said Alice Simms, the tallest of the contestants. "If *she* has trouble getting up again, you know we'll never make it."

"That sidewalk is filthy dirty," Wanda Gay screamed

to her daughter, who was attempting her second backbend. "You're too old for such silliness."

From the second-floor porch, Silly watched the strangers coming up the sidewalk. She saw three party dresses followed by a woman in baggy pants and a man's hat, followed by a boy in a Little League uniform.

"This isn't a place to freshen up!" Miss Fane raised her voice. "Those windows up there have bars on them." Dodging a runaway baton, she turned on Pearl. "Once again, you have tricked me, and I intend to get even with you if it's my last act on earth. That's my promise." She dug into her purse for her lipstick and powder.

"This is such a pretty little town," Pearl said, blowing smoke toward her mother. "I'm already thinking about moving here."

"No you are not," said Miss Fane, pointing her lipstick in Pearl's face. "I forbid you to entertain such a thought as the one you have just now been careless enough to express. Your place is with me and you know it. I am not a well woman by any stretch of the imagination. I happen to be a semi-invalid on the road to becoming totally incapacitated and most certainly will if you don't watch out. Oh Lord, how many times must I be called on to say this before I die."

"Not many more, if we're lucky," said Pearl.

"I knew you'd say that," said Miss Fane.

"I knew you expected it," said Pearl.

"I'd like to live here too," said Little Teddy. "Let's move."

Demeris was about to say the same thing when Wanda Gay stopped her. "Don't you dare copy him," she said lifting a hand. "I'll slap you silly if you do."

"Somebody's talking about me," Silly shouted to her husband, who was still inside.

"Somebody's always talking about you," he shouted back.

"Let me handle this," said Miss Fane, powdering as she walked. "Little Teddy, you need to be straightened out, and I'm just the one to do it. You would not enjoy living here and that's final, so erase that desire from your mind. If Big-Teddy-who-died-in-the-war could hear you wish for such a thing he would disown you for disrespect. Your place is with Pearl and Pearl's place is with me. In other words, Pearl's place and my place are the exact same place. And so is yours."

"I'd still like to live here," said Teddy.

"If you and Pearl moved away from Morehope there would simply be no more hope, not for me anyway," said Wanda Gay. "How would I ever get anything done without you. It would be a tragedy."

"Whose tragedy?" Pearl asked but no one bothered to answer.

While Miss Fane led the way to the jail Pearl lagged behind. She sat down on a bench and motioned for her son to join her.

"It will be impossible to talk to Frank until Mother has said all she intends to say," Pearl told Teddy. "So let's sit here and watch these twirlers. They look like they need an audience."

The twirlers, counting aloud, started their routine from the beginning, while Pearl and Teddy watched. "They're doing a lot of posing and not much twirling," Teddy said to his mother. "I'm not impressed."

"Don't let them hear you," Pearl said, "they've got enough problems as it is."

Juanita Moore, who was called Woo Woo, dropped her baton and instead of picking it up she pantomimed twirling. Then Alice Simms lost her count. Linda Margaret tripped over her feet and Woo Woo, who was slightly overweight, forgot to kneel.

"Awful," said Teddy.

"Not so loud," said his mother.

"We're scheduled to perform for the judges at three o'clock today, and we're not ready." Woo Woo, exploding her insecurity, chose Pearl for a target. "I've only been twirling two months, and Linda Margaret has made this routine too hard for me, and I just hate her for it."

"Start over," Pearl said calmly. "I bet I can help you pull it together."

"Well you certainly can't do any harm," Teddy whispered into his mother's ear, "because they're just terrible. I could do a lot better, and I don't even know how."

"Where did all that confidence come from?" asked Pearl.

"Out of the encyclopedias, I guess," said her son. "That's what Uncle Frank says."

When Pearl got up to help the twirlers reconstruct their routine, Teddy, thinking about the best way to get Frank out of jail, remained on the bench. He was anxious to see his uncle, because he had brought him a present, something that he didn't even want his mother to know about. He intended to ask if he could be alone with Frank for a few minutes and that's when he would give his uncle the gift. He had taken it from his grandfather's old tool chest and was carrying it in his pocket. It was a file, a very old one. Teddy was sure that Frank could use it to saw his way out of jail.

While Pearl worked with the twirlers, Teddy took the file out of his pocket and studied it on both sides. "I sure hope it's strong enough to cut through the bars," he said, "because that's the only way Frank will ever get out. They don't let people go free just because their family is decent-looking. Even I know that."

"Teddy, what's that you're saying?" Pearl spoke over her shoulder. "Are you talking to me?"

"No."

"What are you saying?"

"I'm saying that we are decent people, but we aren't decent-looking, not like *your* mother thinks we are. At least not today we're not. It's going to take more than what we've got to show to get Uncle Frank out of jail."

"Somehow," said Pearl, turning her attention back to the twirlers. "I can't be bothered with any of that right now."

TWENTY-TWO

"Everybody stop right now and help me find my insulin before I have a blackout," Miss Fane moaned. "I can't go another step until I have a shot. Wanda Gay, come here and help me look." She slipped a hard candy into her mouth as she searched her handbag. "Unless Pearl has hidden my syringe, it's right here in my purse."

"I did not bring your medicine, Mother," Pearl said as though talking to the twirlers. "That's not my responsibility."

"Damn you for desiring to kill me." Miss Fane raised her voice. Frank could hear her clearly, but it was Pearl who brought him to his feet.

"I can help you," she told the twirlers. "But you've got to trust me in spite of the fact that I've never twirled a baton in my life and never intend to."

Frank had always been under the spell of his sister's quiet, confident voice. Early on her voice had captured him, found its way into his heart, and remained there like a love poem that could not be forgotten. From one woman to the next, Frank had traced his sister's inflections, her phrases and laughter, but in them he had never found the same quality, only shreds of it.

From the window of his cell, he obliterated his mother's sharp tones, and Wanda Gay's echoes, and heard only Pearl's instructions to the twirlers.

"You don't have to change very much, but you do have to perform with more dignity and confidence."

"If only Father were still alive," Frank said as if Pearl were in the cell with him. "We certainly wouldn't be here. We'd be down at that automobile graveyard. If Father had lived we'd still be helping him."

They had grown up at Albert's feet. Miss Fane had seen to that. "It's time for Frank and Pearl to get out of the house and go bother Albert for a while," she would say. "You're making Wanda Gay and me nervous with all your silly laughing. I believe Albert needs to be pestered today."

Down at the automobile graveyard they would follow their father on his rounds. He was always on the lookout for used parts, especially for his favorite customers: Louise Johnson, the banker's wife, Lucille Wisenbaker, whose husband traveled for a living, and the two widows, Mary Reynolds and Charlotte Whitehead. "I keep their engines roaring," Albert would tell Pearl and Frank. They would walk on either side of him as he made his rounds through the graveyard. While helping him search for batteries or generators or fan belts and windshields that could be used once again, they would listen to him talk about his faithful customers and their particular engine problems.

Not long after Charlotte Whitehead's fatal car accident they came to realize that everything they had ever heard about their father and his special clients was true. They were helping him search for a carburetor for Lucille Wisenbaker when he told them how he operated his business.

"I believe we can take my dear Charlotte Whitehead's carburetor, and transplant it into Lucy's Chevrolet," he had said. "Whitey's been dead for six months, so she won't mind if Lucy has her parts, but Lucy is liable to explode if she finds out she's driving around with something that once belonged to a competitor. They never could get along, and it was all because of me. Always arguing, always competing, always after my attention."

He removed Charlotte Whitehead's carburetor and

made his children promise not to tell Lucille where he got it. He made them promise not to tell Louise that she was driving around with Ivory Miller's hubcaps, and that Mary Reynolds was able to start her engine only because of the spare parts he had taken from Nelda Monroe's Dodge after it had been totaled on the highway.

"Of course, I'm closer to some of these women than others," Albert told Frank and Pearl. "But all of them are mighty jealous of my affection. I have to be careful to avoid trouble. If Annie Pate knew that I took the slack out of her steering wheel with some of the parts I removed from her sister's wreck, she'd be of a mind to kill somebody."

For hours Albert would disappear under the hood of a car, removing or cleaning or replacing parts and Pearl and Frank would be there beside him. They would hold his trouble lamp or hand him tools with the skill of a surgeon's assistant. They could anticipate his thoughts when it came to tools. He never had to ask for anything by name or size. They knew instinctively what he wanted and gave it to him, often without an exchange of words.

Sometimes he would tell them what he was repairing and why. Other times he would talk about whatever happened to be on his mind that day. "I thought your mother was so beautiful that I fell off the roof when I first saw her," he had once said. From his cell Frank could still hear him. "That's how I broke my foot. That's why I can't walk today. I was a victim of beauty. Her beauty is all I saw then. But it's sure hard to see it today."

"It certainly is," Frank said as he edited his mother's voice from the air. He often wondered if he too had been one of beauty's victims. He wondered what course his father's life would have taken had he not fallen off the roof.

After realizing that he would always be lame, speed became Albert's fascination. He followed his brothers from one job to the next, from one town to the next, racing his truck up and down the highways. After taking over the automobile graveyard, he rebuilt cars in his spare time and raced them around his mechanic's shed, making a circle of ruts in the red clay that remained there long beyond his lifetime. He could relax behind the wheel of a speeding car. The faster he could make it go, the clearer his thoughts became, and the closer he felt to something divine inside him. Around and around he would race until every troublesome thought disappeared into a cloud of red dust that could be seen from the town square.

"This is as close as a man can get to flying," he would explain to his favorite customers.

He would race his fast cars only at the graveyard, never on the open highway, and he was not given to what he called practical everyday driving. "That," he said, "is useless, especially for people who have two good legs." He preferred instead to hobble through town. To Miss Fane's disgust he walked everywhere he needed to go.

"All Albert wants to do is call attention to the fact that he's a cripple," she said. "All he wants to do is remind everyone that I'm the cause of it."

On his walks through town, he would make several stops to drink coffee and dispense advice about mechanical problems. "Maybe it's the carburetor," he would say. "Maybe it's the generator. I think I can find you a cheap one. But don't expect anything before noon."

All his customers knew that he devoted his mornings to racing, and his afternoons to repairing by appointment only. And when he had no customers he often spent a few hours teaching Frank and Pearl what they needed to know in order to help him.

"Rotating tires was something that he never liked doing," Frank recalled. He was watching Pearl demonstrate a three-count step to the twirlers. She and Frank had been in charge of rotating the tires. They also changed the oil and on occasion the spark plugs. From time to time Albert would allow them to race one of his cars around the shed.

"We were never the same after that accident," Frank said. Batons were flying like giant sparks to the level of

126

his window. "After that accident we knew too much about each other."

The accident had occurred when they were both in their early teens, long before they were eligible for driver's licenses. "It was as though we exchanged places for a brief time," Frank said, "for only a moment in the face of death we were different. I have never understood what really happened." At times he felt as though he and Pearl had shared the same nightmare, that the auto accident had not actually occurred.

They had been racing through the perfectly formed ruts when Frank lost control of the car. As they rolled over and over he saw a life flashing before him, but it was not his own life, it was Pearl's or it seemed to be Pearl's. He saw the face of the man his sister was to marry, and the face he saw was not unlike his own.

"Just relax," she had said, in that calm voice she always used when speaking to her brother. "This isn't your time. You're going to die someplace far away from here." The car continued to roll. The roof flattened, forcing the two of them onto the floorboard where they were trapped, pressed one against the other.

"Don't worry," Frank had said to his half-conscious sister. "You're going to have to bury us all." His words quickly faded from his memory, but not from Pearl's.

"She should never have married Teddy," Frank said, still watching her from his window. "She should have waited for someone she didn't love so much, someone who was not marked for an early death."

"Don't let her marry a man who looks too much like me," Frank had told his father after the wreck. "He'll make her happy but not for long."

Many times throughout his life Frank was to awaken in the middle of the night with his head swimming and his bed rolling over and over. He would hang on to the sheets, the bedposts, the lamps, anything that seemed remotely stable, and try to relax with the ride. "Just be calm," he would hear Pearl say. "This is one of those moments when there's nothing else you can do."

"Stagger your aerials on counts of four," Pearl shouted. Something in her voice brought Frank back to the moment. "That way you don't have to worry about being together. You can relax a little, and if we're lucky we might even get a smile from one of you."

In her voice Frank was beginning to hear a different tone. Hidden within the softness was a harder sound, one he had not expected to hear. He watched her from the small barred window and for the first time she seemed unfamiliar. She now appeared to be less like him and more like everyone else in his family.

"They're all strangers to me now," he said. He sat on the bed and waited, dreading the sound of footsteps on the stairs.

TWENTY-THREE

Silly Sticks was accustomed to strangers, but there was something singular about these people and she could not decide exactly what it was. Standing between the "Welcome" sign and the chair occupied by her husband's geranium, Silly kept an eye on the visitors as they stopped to search for insulin and needles.

"I can't find my syringe," Miss Fane said, "and now my head is swimming. Somebody find me a soft chair." Wanda Gay forced a piece of candy into her mother's mouth and supported her to the stairs, where she braced herself on the banister and looked up, dreading the climb. There were twelve steps in all leading to the second-floor landing where Silly stood, twisting the ends of a tape measure draped around her neck.

"Today's parade lines up on the other side of town." Silly pointed straight up. "Just ask those twirlers to show you the way." She was wearing a faded blue housecoat and was barefoot.

"We're not here for a parade," said Wanda Gay, reaching into her neckline to pull up a slip strap.

"Oh, now I get it." Silly adjusted her green visor. "You're here to get fitted for new foundation garments to enhance those special outfits you're wearing. My, how my reputation is getting around. I usually go door-to-door to do my fittings, but I sure don't have to. Ladies, come right in here and get saddled up with a brassiere you'll never want to take off again. You'll swear that it just grew on you."

"Brassieres?" From the third step Miss Fane eyed Silly questionably. "We did not come here to buy brassieres."

Silly whipped the tape measure from around her neck and flashed a broad, slightly golden smile. "What is this world coming to," she said. "All of a sudden everybody wants custom-made foundation garments. Once you have one you'll never want anything store-bought again."

"We are not here for a fitting of any kind," Miss Fane replied adamantly. But again Silly ignored her.

"I warn you in advance," she continued. "In order for me to arrive at your true cup size, you ladies will have to remove everything from the waist up, but I can't allow you to do that out here in the open air because it's against the law. My husband works for the law. Best to keep that in mind."

"You're not talking to idiots," said Miss Fane, slowly climbing the stairs.

"You don't say," said Silly, pressing her short fingers to her cheeks.

"Who are you?" asked Wanda Gay.

"Just call me Silly," said the jailer's wife.

"Thank you, I already have," said Miss Fane. She was halfway up the stairs and the candy was beginning to revive her.

"Honey," exclaimed Silly, speaking directly to Frank's mother. "Do you know that I have what they're now calling x-ray vision?" She touched her temples. "Even from way up here I can see straight through your clothes and tell that for an older woman you have two of the most beautiful bosoms I've ever seen, except for Mrs. Eugene Davis who lives right over there." She pointed toward a row of trash cans on the curb.

"I bet you say that to everybody," said Wanda Gay, staring in the direction Silly was pointing.

"If I believe it, I say it," said Silly, stretching out her measuring tape.

"What's going on out here?" Sam Sticks came outside to water his geranium. "You women look like you got all dressed up to tell fortunes."

"Well, we didn't," said Miss Fane.

"They're here to get fitted," said Silly. "Can't you tell?"

"Then make sure they get their money's worth," said Sam. He was slightly overweight, had tiny feet, and was dressed in khakis. Safety pins had been used to replace the screws in his glasses which were resting on his forehead. He was bald and had no eyebrows, but he did have a smile that put Miss Fane at ease.

"Oh, you look kind and sensible, especially around the mouth," she said, climbing the rest of the steps rapidly. "We've come to see my boy Frank. I'm his mother."

"You can't be Frank's mother," said Silly. "We like Frank. Everybody does."

"Frank's free to leave, but he won't," said Sam, ushering the visitors into the office.

Deer heads hung on the walls, along with large-mouth bass and wild boar. "I used to be a taxidermist," he said, pointing to the trophies. "I used to be a hunter, too, but I gave that up because I don't like killing. I just might go back to taxidermy one day though. That's what I've been thinking. I guess I just like preserving things."

"But he likes locking people up best of all," said Silly. "Especially if they're real mean. That's his speciality." She hovered around Miss Fane with the tape measure while her husband explained Frank's situation.

"Frank has a good reputation in this town. He just got confused here for a minute or two, and who wouldn't with a wife like his. You might not think I can sympathize on that level, but I can."

"I believe you," said Miss Fane, casting a hard stare toward the jailer's wife. "Believe me, I do."

"Mother's words are my words," said Wanda Gay. She placed hands of support on her mother's shoulders.

"Mother's words are my words, too," said Demeris

twirling around until the skirt of her evening gown stood straight out.

"What a pretty little girl," said Silly. "She knows how to make a breeze with her skirt."

"Guess what else I can do?" said Demeris.

"Surprise me," said Silly.

"In this family we don't believe in surprises." Miss Fane spoke quickly. "Demeris, come stand by me."

Demeris refused.

"Wanda Gay, make your daughter come stand by me so I can watch out for her."

"I can fit you with a foundation garment that will expand as your little buds grow bigger and bigger," Silly said sweetly. "Judging from the size of the other women in your family, I can tell right off that the day is coming when you will need strong support to maintain a natural uplift."

"Wanda Gay!" Miss Fane raised her voice in alarm. "You make your daughter come stand by me right now. I mean it. I don't want her fitted for *anything*."

"That's what they all say at first," said Silly. "But after a week of upper body comfort, everyone comes back for more."

Wanda Gay jerked Demeris by the arm and led her to Miss Fane, who was sitting in a chair with Longhorn arm rests. "You stand right here by Mother, and don't you move," Wanda Gay said.

Miss Fane put her arms around Demeris to hold her in place.

"Last night we left Morehope immediately after my piano recital," she explained. "That's why we're all dressed up. You must believe me." She was staring directly into Sam's face, but still speaking for the benefit of his wife. "We did not come here to buy brassieres. If we had wanted some brassieres we'd have stayed in Morehope."

"We can buy them there," said Demeris as if she expected no one to believe her.

"My goodness," said Silly, pressing her fingers to her round cheeks. "I didn't know that. Where's Morehope?"

"Texas," said Demeris. "Why don't you come visit us sometime?"

"I just might," said Silly.

"We haven't had visitors in ten years." Miss Fane pinched Demeris's arm to shut her up. "Now if I may finish what I started without another interruption—we have come to take Frank home. That's why we're here."

"Oh yes, Frank," said Sam. "I almost forgot about Frank."

"Well, we haven't," said Miss Fane.

"Bud Johnson had no intention of pressing charges or getting Frank into trouble," Sam explained. "He just called a police officer to settle your boy down and keep him off the highways. But when Frank pointed his shotgun in the officer's face, we had no choice but to take him in. We're holding him on a $500 bail, which his company has already offered to post. Only thing is, Frank refuses to accept it. I've never had a prisoner yet who felt like he was better off in jail."

"I'll pay the bail myself," announced Miss Fane. "Frank will accept money from his mother. He always has. But all of us have a problem accepting anything from outside the family. We're just that close, you know."

She took out her checkbook, but before she started to write, she spoke up again. Her tone was confidential. "I am not prepared to make this check payable to some county jail or to a total stranger. If I do that, the people down at the Morehope Bank will think all kinds of things they've never thought of before. So I'll just make it payable to Sears and Roebuck and you can figure out some way of cashing it."

"That's just fine," said Silly. "Mrs. Fort Smith who works at Sears and Roebuck up in Pine Bluff," she pointed to the light fixture on the ceiling, "well, she's a very agreeable customer of mine. She's about the same size as your daughter here, and she'll do anything I ask."

"I bet she will too," Miss Fane said. She finished writing the check. Silly put it in the pocket of her housecoat, and Sam took the visitors upstairs to see Frank. On the way up, Miss Fane whispered to Wanda Gay, "Be sure you keep an eye on Demeris. I'll tell you why later."

TWENTY-FOUR

Out on the lawn, Pearl was still working with the three twirlers. "What's wrong with you, all of you," she said. "You look like you're about half-way alive. You must look energetic and eager. No one will pay any attention to you if you don't." She asked them to reverse some movements so the hardest parts came first and the easiest were then made to appear harder by adding some fast footwork.

Teddy, sitting on the bench, occasionally added his say. "That doesn't look right Mother," he said when the twirlers tried to perform a new series of steps Pearl had made up. "Don't make them do that."

"Who's doing this? You or me?" Pearl asked. "Please keep quiet until I'm through, and then I'll ask for your opinion."

"Well, it doesn't look right," he said again. "You should take my word for it right now, not later."

Turning her back on her son, Pearl addressed the twirlers again. "There are days when I can't please anyone, including my own son. Everybody thinks they can tell me what to do."

"All I want is a gold medal," said Woo Woo. "I swear, my mother will kill me if we don't win one."

"Then we better get busy," said Pearl, rearranging the girls in the line, so the tallest, Alice Simms, was in the center. "It's hard to sit back and watch somebody doing something that could stand to be improved upon. It's especially hard when you see clearly what's wrong."

"Exactly what *is* wrong?" asked Linda Margaret.

"The ending," said Pearl. "You'll never win a first-place medal with an easy ending. The old one isn't any good, and the new one you just made up is even worse. I've seen both of them at every half-time I've ever suffered through. Now let me help you change it. I'm not a twirler but I know how it should look."

"We can't change it again!" cried Woo Woo.

"All we've done is change it," said Alice, who at the age of sixteen was secretly engaged to be married. "Now, we can't even remember it the way it was."

"So how do you expect us to change it again and remember it?" Woo Woo, whose hair was in pincurls, was already confused.

"We can't," said Linda Margaret, the smallest and most energetic of the three and whose aerials were the highest. "I say we'd better try to work with what we've got before we go learning something else."

"Stop fighting me when I'm trying to help you," said Pearl. "You have nothing to lose by starting over, because you certainly won't win a medal with the ending you're doing right now." After rearranging the last steps and twirls, she asked the twirlers to run through the ending again and to pretend they were performing for the judges.

"I'm the judges," Little Teddy said. "Look at me. I won't make faces."

The twirlers ran through the first change, each dropping her baton.

"Start over," Pearl said.

"I hate it when we have to change things around," said Woo Woo. "How's this going to help me when I get to nursing school?"

"You sound like you're old and set in your ways," said Pearl. "That's no way to be. You're still young."

"But I'm too fat to pass this baton around my waist the way you want me too," said Woo Woo.

"Nonsense," said Pearl. "Stretch."

With a grimace Woo Woo passed the baton around her waist without making a drop.

"Good," said Pearl. "Now pass the baton around your right ankle and step back into three pinwheels or whatever you call them, and then salute the judges."

"But I'm scared of the judges," said Alice. "Is it okay if I close my eyes when I salute?"

"All eyes open," commanded Pearl. "You don't want people to think you're sleeping your way through life."

"I can think of worse things," said Alice with a seductive tone.

"Keep your mind on your salute and nothing else," said Pearl, "and remember to hold it for three counts. The judges will think you're finished but you're not. What's coming up is a twelve-count finale, starting with Woo Woo."

"No," said Woo Woo. "I have a bad memory. Start with someone else. You think I'm Einstein, don't you?"

"I assure you," said Pearl. "Einstein is the last person who comes to mind right now."

"It's even too hard for me, and I'm the best," said Linda Margaret.

"It's too hard only if you fight it," said Pearl. "You can't think about how hard something is. You'll get all stiff and paralyzed if you do."

"But it's scary," said Alice Simms.

"Then what you do is brainwash yourself," Pearl advised. "Just say over and over, 'This isn't scary, it's just new.' Take it from me, anything new seems terrifying at first. Now run through it again and again as many times as it takes until the newness wears off. My son sitting right over there is the judge. Twirl to him."

The twirlers stumbled through the new ending, and Pearl made them do it over several times.

"We'll never learn all this before the parade," said Woo Woo.

"Then you won't be in the parade," said Pearl. "You

have to get your priorities straight, and this goes for *everything,* not just twirling. First things first."

While the twirlers practiced under Pearl's careful eye, Marsha paraded down the sidewalk on her way to visit Frank. She was dressed in tight black peddlepushers and a white, see-through blouse of crinkled nylon over a red foundation garment that testified to Silly's skill with a tape measure.

Neither Pearl nor her son noticed Marsha prancing up the steps with a car-hop tray balanced on the palm of her hand. A hamburger and a milkshake in a paper cup were riding on the tray along with napkins weighted down by a bottle of ketchup. Straws were sticking out of her blond hair held in place with black bobbie pins and tortoise-shell combs.

As Marsha disappeared inside the jail, Pearl, still keeping a close eye on the twirlers, sat down next to her son, the judge. "You give other people very good advice, Mother," he said. "When we move away from Morehope, you could get a great job just helping people with their problems."

"And who's going to help me with mine?" Pearl asked.

"I guess I will," said Teddy. "You certainly don't have anybody else."

TWENTY-FIVE

At the top of the stairs Sam Sticks leaned against a steel
door that slowly swung open with a long steady squeak.
The smell of Old Spice filled the upper hallway.

"That's Frank," said Miss Fane. "He always did use
too much perfume. I never could keep him out of mine."
She rushed into her son's open cell. A radio was playing
in a corner. An army bed was neatly made, and cigarette
butts were scattered on the floor.

Frank was sitting in a straightback chair and staring
through the window at a patch of cloudless sky. "I was
wondering how long it would take you to get here," he
said. His back was turned to his mother.

"It's time for you to come home, Frankie," Miss Fane
said.

"Not this time," Frank answered. "I'm sitting right
here until I figure out what to do with myself. If it takes
me from now until next year, my time will be well spent."
He stood up and turned around. His face was no longer
lean but round. His small eyes danced about, and his lips
seemed to stretch all the way across his face. His long
nose was his most noticeable feature.

"Oh, Frankie," Miss Fane cried. "You look more like
your father than ever. Why has it come to this? You look
so much like Albert I just can't stand looking at you. You
didn't used to favor him so bad."

"Demeris," shouted Wanda Gay. "This is exactly what

your grandfather looked like at the very last. Now come see, darling. You were just a baby when he died."

"You don't look like yourself, Uncle Frank," Demeris said.

"That kind of thing runs in Albert's bloodline," Miss Fane explained "When I married him I thought he was one person and the day after Frank was born I woke up and realized that Albert was somebody entirely different. I have never heard of anyone changing so fast. Suddenly he looked just like a toad and acted like one too. That's when I started talking about the necessity of separation. Every married couple needs to be separated from time to time. Isn't that right, Wanda Gay?"

"Yes, Mother," Wanda Gay replied.

"So it wasn't your allergy to cat hair and motor oil after all," said Frank. "Why exactly did you and Daddy marry, Mother? I want to hear it again."

"For your information," said Miss Fane. "I had to make certain sacrifices to marry Albert. My father didn't want me to marry him, but I did it anyway. I married Albert for you children."

"Are you trying to say that we were already born?" Frank asked.

"No, Frank," Wanda Gay replied with a tight frown. "Mother isn't trying to say that at all. Listen with both your ears and you'll know what Mother is trying to say."

"No, you weren't already born," said Miss Fane. "How dare you make such an insinuation. I knew you were going to be born. I knew that my father expected you to be born, and I knew that Albert would build us a big white house to live in. My father certainly wasn't going to leave me his house, so I had to come up with someplace decent to live."

"A decent place to live," said Marsha, parading into the cell. "That's always been my problem too."

"What's she doing here?" Miss Fane threw hateful eyes on Frank's wife.

"This room looked a lot better when I lived in it,"

140

said Marsha, avoiding eye contact with Frank's family. "It smelled a lot better too." Hooking the car-hop tray on the back of a chair and moving it in front of Frank, she told him that she was first going to feed him, and then she was going to take him home. "I know how to take care of you now, Frankie," she whispered sweetly. "And that's just what I'm going to do, now that I have a new job."

"Taking care of Frank is my business," said Miss Fane. "Not yours."

"Why Miss Fane, honey, I didn't see you standing there, not really," Marsha whined, pretending total surprise. "For the first time in your life, you were almost invisible, weren't you? How did that happen?"

"Frank's coming home with me, where he belongs." Miss Fane stepped forward. "I'm the one who knows what he needs."

"Let's let Frankie make that choice," said Marsha, winking at her husband. "He's a man who knows what he likes."

"I'm staying right here," Frank said. "Going one place is about as bad as the other."

"I refuse to believe that you mean that," said Miss Fane.

"You need to come home so Mother and Pearl can feed you and take care of you and watch after you," said Wanda Gay.

"You only have one home," said Demeris. "And that's the one you better go to."

"Frankie!" said Marsha, sashaying over to the window. "If you stand right here in front of this tiny, little window, you can see the Tall Pine Drive-in where, day before yesterday, I took a job as a car-hop." She rolled her eyes seductively as she spoke. "You'll be able to watch me every time I serve a carload of good-looking men, and that will help you decide which home to go to. It won't take you long to realize that being in the public eye has done me a world of good. I feel like a movie star every time I go to work, and that feeling has made me a more thoughtful person." She strutted around the cell as though modeling a new personality. Then Miss Fane took her place in front of the window.

"Frankie!" Miss Fane said, talking with her eyes. "If you stand right here in front of this tiny little window, you can also see Pearl's car, which is parked out front. I'm going out there right now, and I'm going to sit down in that car, and I'm going to go on sitting there for as long as it takes for you to come to your senses. I'll be there when you decide to come home, if you don't let me die first."

Miss Fane left the cell while Marsha strutted about, stopping now and then to pose before following her mother-in-law out the door. Then Wanda Gay took her turn at the window.

"Frankie," she said, talking with eyes, "as you know, I have always followed Mother's good example on matters such as this. I don't know what I would do without her in my life, and I pray to God I'll never have to face that situation any time soon because I'd be completely and hopelessly lost and wouldn't know which way to turn." She stared at her hands as she spoke. She had chosen her left index finger for the cameo ring. She didn't know why she had chosen that finger but she was confident that it was the right one. "Now this is what I intend to do," she continued, gazing at her gloved fingers. "I will follow Mother out to the curb, and I will sit down in that car of Pearl's, and I will go on sitting down in that car of Pearl's until you come to your senses. I will also be praying for you the entire time. I have come to believe deeply in prayer, Frank. It can change things."

Wanda Gay left the cell with her hands folded and her head reverently bowed. Then Demeris, pulling up her strapless bodice, took her place at the window.

"Uncle Frank," Demeris said, "If I were you, I'd come back home to Morehope where you can be with people who will help you get to know yourself."

Emulating her mother's prayerful attitude, Demeris

left the cell. The skirt of her formal swept cigarette butts, shoe laces, and gum wrappers down the hall.

TWENTY-SIX

Frank closed the door to his cell and leaned against it. He was relieved to be alone. At first the cell had given him a feeling of safety. "I'll be able to sit down and think here," he'd told himself. "This is where I'll be able to decide what to do next." The first night he had slept without waking until the sun poured through the little square window and onto his face. The bed he had slept on reminded him of the cot that had been in Albert's shop. He had often slept there to escape Wanda Gay's whining, his mother's piano students, and the constant ticking of the metronome.

"Most of my visitors don't get this kind of treatment," Sam had said that morning when he brought Frank a cup of coffee and a paper. "But you're different. You're free to go any time you want."

"Not just yet," Frank said. "I have some thinking I need to do first."

After Sam left the cell Frank lay back down and stared at the ceiling. Safe here, he kept thinking while the shaft of sunlight gradually left his face and moved across the bed. For the rest of the day he watched the square of light inch its way across the floor, over his shoes, over the only chair in the room and gradually climb the opposite wall. "I wonder," he said, "just how long I can stay here."

The cell had seemed large at first, but as the day came to an end, the space began to shrink. The thick walls

144

enclosed Frank like a suit of armor that had shrunk with its wearer inside it. He turned on the one light, a 25-watt bulb that gave the walls the appearance of yellowed paper and seemed to inhibit the shrinking.

With a dull pencil he wrote his name on the wall above his bed. Other names and addresses had been scribbled there, along with deathbed confessions and Bible verses. Above the window someone had drawn a universe of stars, moons, and planets surrounding a small red dot labeled: The Earth.

The drawing reminded Frank of his father and the steel reinforced Plymouth Albert had given him to drive. Albert had redesigned the car to be accident-proof and Frank wondered what had happened to it. "If I could only find that reinforced Plymouth," he said. "Then everything would be all right again."

After their accident the Plymouth was the only car Albert would allow Frank or Pearl to use. Before he turned it over to them he designed a second roof of steel to be supported by lead pipes. With his welder's torch he went to work crisscrossing strips of steel over the top of the car. He wove the strips together like the crust of a pie and on top of that latticework he fastened another layer of steel around which he attached a rim of chrome. He burned the names Frank and Pearl into the top of the car, and around the names he burned stars, clouds, and ringed planets. "I got carried away and drew the whole damn universe on top of this car," Albert said. "You kids can drive this thing as fast as you want to. It's perfectly safe. You can turn over and over I don't care how many times and the worst that can happen to you will be a bump on your head."

Frank raced the Plymouth alone or with his sister, and no matter how many times he lost control of the wheel the car would not turn over. The heavy roof anchored it to the earth.

"You're a terrible influence on our children." Miss Fane, standing outside Albert's shop, shook her fist at her husband. It was the only time she had visited Albert's place of business. "Fast cars and fast women. That's all you study. When are you going to get some dignity into your life. I didn't marry you to be a hot-rodder."

"But I am a hot-rodder," Albert shouted. Sparks flew from his welder's torch. "Too bad you can't find a use for hot-rods."

On hearing of Albert's death, the barber, Lou Reed, said that Albert loved two things: cars and women, not necessarily in that order. "He couldn't walk very fast," said Lou, "but he sure got around, if you know what I mean. Every story he told on himself was true. Not many people know that."

Every Friday Albert had visited Lou Reed's barber shop for a haircut and a shave. He refused to shave more than once a week and he refused to shave himself. "A man has to have some luxury in his life," he would say if questioned about the way he lived. "I've got several, and they all got pretty names too. You want to know who they are, I guess?"

"Don't name names in my shop, Albert," Lou Reed would say. "You'll cause me to lose all my customers."

"I've had every woman in Morehope that's worth having," the lame mechanic would boast during his Friday afternoon visits to the barber shop. "I've repaired every kind of engine you can imagine. You might not think I've got that sort of ability but I have. Comes natural to cripples."

Albert saw no reason to stop racing his cars or taking his lady customers on breath-taking spins around the mechanics shop. One at a time he would drive them around the shed first at a slow speed and then faster and faster until they screamed with fright, begged him to slow down. Housewives whose husbands had long since tired of them would visit Albert with the most minor problems, a broken windshield wiper, a radio antenna, or a hubcap that needed replacing.

"You need your battery recharged," he would say to

Lucille, Louise, or Mary Reynolds, his most faithful customers. "That's going to take some time so we might as well take a joy ride while we wait." With one of them strapped into the passenger's seat of a souped-up wreck he would circle the tin mechanic's shed gradually building speed until he had floored the accelerator. He would then send the car jumping the deep ruts and steer a steady path toward another shed, a more secluded one, where he claimed only certain repairs could be made.

Louise Johnson was always certain that her repair work would need to be done in the small shed. At least once a week she had telephoned Albert with a problem involving her ignition. "Something's wrong," she would say in a breathless voice. "I think it's my starter again."

"Creep on down here, Ouise," Albert would tell her. "Starters are my speciality, but you know that already. I've fixed your starter so many times now, I suppose I'll eventually have to replace it."

"No, not yet," Louise would plead. "Just patch me up for the time being."

Louise considered herself Albert's most devoted customer. She often washed his clothes, brought him food and old magazines to read in his spare time. "I know there are other women in your life," she would say, "but don't tell me who they are. As long as I can half-way believe I'm the only one, that's all that matters."

Albert had instructed his special customers to call up first to make sure he was available. He would patiently listen to their problems and make the necessary repairs. Then on Friday afternoons he would deliver invoices for work well done to their husbands who congregated in Lou Reed's barber shop. There they would encourage him to boast of his amorous adventures. They would listen to stories of his nameless conquests, but coming from a lame mechanic who was often unwashed, and unshaven, and smelled of motor oil and cats, they found his stories impossible to believe.

"I'd better send my wife over to you Albert," Sam

Wisenbaker, the county clerk, would say with a deep laugh. "She's getting too much for me to handle."

For longer than Albert could remember Lucille Wisenbaker had come to him complaining of her noisy transmission. "My gears are sticking again," she would say, and Albert always knew how to solve her problem.

With the widow Mary Reynolds it was the same. She said she would be lost without Albert's constant eye on her engine. "It's my radiator," she would complain, even on the coldest days of winter. "It's boiling over. Do something, Albert. I know you can help me."

"It is simply a disgrace," Miss Fane shouted to her husband on the only day she had ever set foot in the automobile graveyard. "Here you are servicing all the tired worn-out women of this county. What kind of a brothel do you think you're running anyway?"

"A damn good one," Albert said. "They come to me with simple problems and I patch them up and deliver a bill. What's wrong with that?"

"Plenty," Miss Fane screamed. "You've got Frank idolizing your every move. Thank God, Wanda Gay is on my side, but Pearl, what's to become of Pearl? Lord only knows what effect all this will have on a girl of her age."

Like her brother, Pearl felt safe at the automobile graveyard. To her it was a peaceful place far removed from the fracas of her mother's daily life. For hours she would watch her father bringing wrecked cars back to life again. Sometimes he would sell them. Sometimes he would keep them. Sometimes he would ask his favorite daughter what to do. "Should we keep this one?" he would ask. And Pearl would always say, "Let's take a fast ride in it before we make up our minds."

She was more comfortable in the automobile graveyard than anywhere else. It was a silent place. She could think there. Among the wreckage she would read for hours, or daydream, or wander aimlessly through the maze. The smell of used motor oil would forever remind her of her father and the Plymouth he had reinforced with steel. She had felt safe in that car, safer than any car she had ever driven and so had Frank.

Since leaving home, Frank had searched for that feeling of safety. In his cell he expected to find it again. He had expected to be protected from the outside world, but he soon realized that his hopes were too high.

Down the hall he could hear his mother screaming at Marsha, and outside he could hear Pearl shouting instructions to the twirlers. He watched her from the window. Big Teddy's blazer was slung over one shoulder, and the man's hat was pushed back on her head. Little Teddy was still sitting on the bench.

"That's just like Pearl," Frank said. "Always doing something for someone else."

In his last hour, collapsed on a street in Rio while Carnival floats drifted by like apparitions from a life he had never lived, Frank was to lift his head from the pavement and see a woman in a blazer who looked like his sister. "What are you doing here," he said to the woman, who was silently laughing. On realizing she was a total stranger he wondered why he had not come to Brazil much earlier in his life. He wondered why he could not hear the woman's laughter and what Pearl was doing at that moment. If only he could hear her voice, feel her hand on his chest, he would be able to go on breathing. He was sure of it.

But watching his sister from the window of his cell he had no premonition of his early death.

"Mother, wait for me!" Wanda Gay cried.

"She has a voice that could slice steel," Frank said. "If Pearl and I had only known we were creating a monster, I'm sure we'd have been nice to Wanda Gay. It would have been well worth the trouble, but we didn't know that then."

"Don't give up," Pearl shouted to the twirlers. "You're not finished until you're finished. Stop trying to pretend you are when you're not."

"She's beginning to sound like Mother," Frank said.

Alice Simms had given up and sat down on the grass, and Pearl was forcing her to her feet again. "It's not difficult." She shook a finger in the twirler's face. "You just think it is. It's nothing but a waltz step speeded up. It looks different but it's just the same as always. Now get up from there! Do you think I'm doing this for my mental health? Do you think I have time to waste on you or what?"

"I've got to get out of here," Frank said. "I've got to go some place far away before I start sounding like Mother too. If it can happen to Pearl it can happen to anyone."

He wanted to go to a place where he couldn't understand a word of the language. He didn't want to hear any more opinions, especially opinions about what he should or should not be doing.

"But where?" he wondered, circling the cell. It was fourteen paces long on each side. The walls were thick and damp and the window bars refused to give, but the door was unlocked and standing open. Frank felt as though the entire world could walk in unannounced. "That's not exactly what I had expected," he said. He knew it was time to leave. But he didn't know where to go. "Some place far away," he said. "Some place where no one knows my name."

TWENTY-SEVEN

"Take your hands off me this instant," Miss Fane demanded. Her voice, traveling into Frank's cell, melded with Pearl's instructions to the twirlers. "Take your hands off your hips on the count of three. Now! This instant. This is a nine-count phrase. Nine counts is all you've got. Break it down into groups of threes."

"Five seconds," Miss Fane said in a harsh whisper. "You have five seconds to take your hands off me before I slap you."

"Mother, are you all right?" Wanda Gay asked.

Frank's heart was racing. All the air seemed to have left the cell and for the first time in years he struggled to take a deep breath.

"You slut!" Miss Fane screamed. "You are every decent man's downfall."

"God, don't let them come back up here," Frank prayed. "If only I could lock this door from the inside, I would."

Miss Fane was on the landing between the cells and the second-floor offices. Marsha was gripping her elbow. Wanda Gay and Demeris were watching from the top of the stairs.

"I said take your filthy hands off me this instant, you disgusting woman. I need my insulin. I'm dizzy. I'm weak. I'm very, very weak and you are not making matters any easier. People like you never do."

Marsha did not loosen her grip. "You think I'm working against you, but I'm not," she said. "I love Frank as much as you do, if not more. And if he decides to go back home with you, I want to go with him. That's all I ask. I know deep in your heart you want me to be with him too, Mom."

Miss Fane flinched on the word *Mom*.

"I hope you don't mind if I call you that," Marsha said. Her breath smelled of menthol cigarettes and Listerine. "I never had a mother who understood me, but if I had to pick, I'd pick one just like you."

"You think I can't see straight through you, don't you?" said Miss Fane. "You think I'm going to let you come to my home and lay up in bed and sleep half the day while I feed you, and clothe you, and wait on you like I wait on Frank, but I'm not. You make me ashamed to be a woman. You make me so ashamed I could die. Only I don't know if I'm ashamed for you or ashamed for me."

"What's the difference?" asked Marsha. "Frank has always said that you and I have ways that are just alike, and out of all of his wives I'm the only one you would end up liking in the long run."

"He never said any such thing," said Miss Fane. "I raised him better than that." Bracing herself on the banister, she felt as though Marsha had stolen her last breath.

"Leave her alone, Marsha," Wanda Gay said as she repinned her wilted corsage. She was still standing at the top of the stairs. "Mother, are you all right? You look so pale all of a sudden. I'm worried about you."

"No I am not all right," Miss Fane gasped. "I happen to be a sugar diabetic invalid. Pearl didn't give me a chance to take my insulin this morning and my head is swimming again."

"Let me help you, *Mom*," said Marsha.

"You wench!" Miss Fane, suddenly regaining strength, slapped Marsha in the face.

"That doesn't make me love you any the less," Marsha said, bracing herself against the wall.

Miss Fane staggered to the bottom of the stairs where Silly was waiting for her. "I'm ready to take your measurements now," she said, harnessing Frank's mother with the tape measure. "Let me take you into the bathroom for a minute, just the two of us, it won't hurt a bit."

"DON'T TOUCH ME!" Miss Fane screamed, beating Silly with her purse. "I'm not like you, and I'm not like her either." She pointed to Marsha, who was running down the stairs with her arms outstretched.

"Oh Mom, just let me throw my arms around you and make everything all right again," Marsha said. "You'll learn to love me the same way you love Frank. I just know you will."

"Get away from me," Miss Fane hissed. Flinging her arms left and right, she ran backwards toward the second-floor exit. Marsha and Silly were close behind. "My life is over. I'm going to take off this cameo ring right now, so help me I am. Wanda Gay, it's almost yours."

"Oh Mother," Wanda Gay said. "I will never be able to fill your shoes. I will never be able to hold the family together. Not the way you do."

Descending the stairs to the second floor, Wanda Gay quickly removed her white gloves. "Oh no!" she said turning on her daughter. "Why didn't I get a manicure before we left home? Why did you let me forget? Demeris, you know how I depend on you to tell me these things. My hands are so ugly today of all days, and it's all your fault too."

TWENTY-EIGHT

Perdita Ogletree-Fane had worn the cameo on her left index finger because it was the only finger on which the ring would fit. Miss Winnie, standing over Frank's Brazilian coffin, confirmed this. Miss Winnie said that Cleopatra Smith was the judge's downfall but that no one in Morehope could blame him at the time. "She was THE most beautiful," Miss Winnie said. "THE most beautiful woman this town has ever known. And besides that she possessed charm and bearing and regal dignity. I don't know what you call this quality today but back then we said *presence*. She had what in those days was called *presence*. Perdita had *presence* too, but Cleopatra Smith had *exotic presence*. You could not take your eyes off her. Even when her swollen ankles were tied up with rags, she made you think she was wearing glass slippers."

"What ever happened to her?" asked Pearl.

"After her feet got bad, she was sent to the attic to darn curtains and socks and wait for the judge to come home," Miss Winnie said. "A new housekeeper was hired to take her place downstairs. I forget her name. She was a woman with big feet and good strong arches but Perdita didn't like her."

"I don't want her waiting on me," she would say. "Where is my dearest Cleopatra?"

"Then the judge would remind her, 'Cleopatra's ankles are weak, my dear.' He always called Perdita, *my dear*.

154

Never did I hear him call her by name. Then Perdita would say, 'Bless *dear* Cleopatra and her swollen ankles. I do hope they aren't too painful.' The next thing we knew Perdita was out of bed and dressed in her brightest colors. 'It's time to restore laughter to this house,' she announced. 'We're going to have a party.' "

The party she gave was, Miss Winnie remembered, the very last one given in that house before it was turned into the county library. Perdita, giving everyone the impression that her period of mourning was over and that her mental health was taking a turn for the better, joyfully prepared for the event. Every day she dressed in spring colors, but when choosing her party dress she selected black silk trimmed with the deepest purple.

The food was prepared by the new housekeeper and Cleopatra was placed in charge of arranging the buffet table. "I insist that you wear one of my most colorful dresses," Perdita said to Cleopatra. "After all, you are one of the family." Perdita chose a dress of scarlet silk and Cleopatra wore it with pride. Turning her head gracefully on her long neck, she wandered among the guests without speaking. No one ever knew quite what to say to her nor she to them.

After she had arranged the table with glazed hams and baked turkeys and fresh breads, fruits, pies and cakes, she stood to one side of the room while Perdita inspected the platters of food.

"Something is missing," she exclaimed. "Where is my special dish? Has anyone seen it?"

While the guests stood around the table waiting for the signal to begin, Perdita disappeared into the kitchen and returned quickly with a silver platter.

"Perhaps you should be the one to serve this delicacy," she told her husband as she placed the platter on the table.

"Just what is this?" the judge asked, but his wife was gliding away through the crowded room. She squeezed Miss Winnie's hand as she passed.

"What is it?" replied Perdita as she ascended the stairs. There was no emotion in her voice, nor sparkle in her vacuous eyes fixed upon her husband. "Why, Miss Cleopatra Smith's silk stockings, of course. Miss Smith's silk stockings stuffed with wild rice, mushrooms, and garnished with garters and plums. Miss Cleopatra Smith has the most delicious ankles. I have heard my husband say this so very often. I am sure you will all enjoy them as much as he."

With all eyes on her she slowly climbed to the top of the stairs. "Miss Cleopatra Smith is quite a special woman in this household," she said, removing the cameo ring from her index finger. "Therefore, Miss Smith, I believe this should belong to you." Perdita threw the ring to Cleopatra's feet. And while the guests watched the ring rolling across the floor, Perdita, leaning on the banister, allowed herself to fall.

"I knew something was wrong by the way she squeezed my hand when she walked across the room." Miss Winnie griped both of Pearl's hands. "Her squeeze was desperate. And besides, she didn't look a bit like herself that night. The next thing I knew everybody was gasping. I looked up and down she came. It seemed to me like it took her the longest time to fall."

"I know what you mean," Pearl said. "I have experienced such a moment."

She stood in front of her brother's coffin, her old English teacher at her side, and listened to the ticking of the wall clock. She walked Miss Winnie back to the waiting car and the ticking followed her.

"I can show you the very square of parquet where she hit her head," Miss Winnie said before getting into the car. "For a long time everyone was stunned. No one moved or made a sound and then that beautiful mulatto picked up the cameo ring and handed it over to Eugenia, who ran upstairs. After that Cleopatra Smith was never seen around here again, and not too many years later the judge died of heart failure."

TWENTY-NINE

Out on the lawn Pearl and Teddy were sitting on the bench while the twirlers practiced for the competition. They had run through their entire routine several times and were still having trouble remembering it.

"People don't like changes, even changes for the better," Pearl said to her son. "That's what I'm finding out. Those twirlers have gotten used to doing things one way and they want to stay with what they already know."

"Because it's comfortable," said Teddy. "They feel secure with the familiar, Mother."

"Oh my God," said Pearl. "What's going to become of you. You're much too young to be talking this way."

"I'm not worried about me," Teddy said. "I'm worried about that Woo Woo girl. She's a lunatic for sure. She'll never learn her new part by this afternoon."

"She'll learn it when she gets ready to," said Pearl, "and not a minute before either."

As if something had forced her to turn her head, Pearl looked up in time to see Miss Fane standing on the high porch and shaking her fist at Silly and Marsha. Wanda Gay and Demeris were fighting to be the next one through the door, and Sam Sticks was trying to edge his way around them.

"Everybody get away from me," Miss Fane said, walking backward toward the geranium on its chair. Her voice was very weak. "I'm not well. I've never been well.

I don't care if I'm ever well again. That's why I'm about to take this cameo off my finger once and for all." Struggling to remove the ring, she took a step backward and tripped over the chair. The geranium fell to the floor and Miss Fane fell onto the banister. For a moment she seemed to regain her balance. She stood up, hurled the ring at Wanda Gay's feet, and then she turned around quickly as if to take a step, but instead she leaned over the banister and allowed herself to fall.

Throwing her purse into the air, she spread her arms as though flying, and for what seemed like eternity to Pearl, although it was no more than a few seconds, Miss Fane hovered over the sidewalk and gardenia bushes. Her purse, lipstick, compact, and kleenex went flying over the front lawn. For a moment it was as though she had done the impossible. Pearl was almost convinced that her mother had indeed conquered the air.

"Mother! Don't do me this way," screamed Wanda Gay chasing the ring down the stairs. "I'm not ready to take your place because I'm still me. I just thought I was ready, but I'm not. I never will be."

"Grandmother," cried Demeris. She followed her mother down the stairs. "Don't do us this way. Not when we need you so bad. Uncle Frank won't come home, and Aunt Pearl won't leave home. Mother's not ready to be you and I'm not ready to be Mother."

Face up, Miss Fane lay motionless on the sidewalk. A halo of blood circled her head, and her blue hair, hardly disturbed by the fall, took on a purplish glow against the dark red.

Silly and Sam, peering silently over the banister, felt they had just witnessed something that had not actually happened. Wanda and Demeris, now on the ground, stared at Miss Fane as though they did not recognize her.

"Oh my God," said Pearl. She stood up quickly. "I don't believe this."

"Don't believe what?" her son asked. He was still

watching the twirlers. "This is their best time yet," he said without looking around. "They just might make it."

Pearl turned her face away from the scene, and tried to focus on the flashing batons. "I just don't believe it," she said, almost choking on her words. "I never really believed it would ever happen."

"Why not?" answered her son. He was only half listening to himself. His eyes were on the twirlers and his heart was in his throat. They had come to the new ending and so far no one had made a mistake. Teddy counted aloud. Pearl stared into space. The twirlers performed the up tempo waltz steps to horizontal spins. Batons flashed around necks, legs, and waists. Horizontal spins became front two-hand spins which led the trio into pinwheels and then their false salutes, their staggered aerials, and their final salute, which they performed to the count.

"Okay girls," said Linda Margaret, "let's prove it to ourselves that this was no accident. Let's do it again."

"I can't believe I didn't make a drop," said Woo Woo.

"Neither can I," said Alice Simms.

"Are you talking about yourself or are you talking about me?" asked Woo Woo. "If you're talking about me, I resent what you just said."

"Stop arguing," said Teddy, "and start over."

A heavy silence fell over the lawn as the twirlers began their routine from the top. Even Teddy noticed the heaviness in the air, but he, like the twirlers, was too preoccupied to stop and look around.

"Teddy," Pearl said. "There's been an accident. Your grandmother has fallen."

"Where?" Teddy said as if just waking up.

In front of the jail a small crowd was gathering, and somewhere on the other side of town a siren could be heard coming closer and closer.

"You must stay here." Pearl held her son's hands tightly. "I don't want you going any closer."

In silence they stood on the bench and watched the crowd gather and the ambulance arrive. A doctor arrived with it. He examined Miss Fane. Then she was placed on a stretcher and her body covered with a sheet.

Silly was still peering over the banister where Miss Fane had fallen, and Sam was trying to force his geranium back into its broken pot. Wanda Gay was sitting on the ground with her face in her hands and the cameo ring in her lap. Demeris was sitting beside her, and Frank, framed by the second-floor portal, was looking down on the scene. In the distance, batons were flying.

"He didn't need the file after all," Teddy said.

"What are you talking about," Pearl managed to say.

"Oh nothing," said her son.

Trembling, Pearl sat back down on the bench and watched the twirlers.

"She's dead, isn't she?" asked Teddy.

"Yes," answered his mother.

Wanda Gay and Demeris got into the ambulance. Teddy watched them. And when the ambulance sped away he asked his mother if it was all right not to feel sad about what had happened.

"I don't know," Pearl said.

"Everybody's got to die sometime," Teddy said, "and she was always praying for God to take her."

"Do you think she really meant that?" Pearl asked.

"Well, when you put it that way, I'm forced to answer no," said Teddy. "But it's easier for us to believe that she was ready to die, so that's what I'm going to believe right now. I do know that she was ready to get rid of us. I'm just not too sure we're ready to get rid of her."

"What do you mean?" his mother asked.

"Well, you know, Mother. It's like being locked up and then all at once you can go free, and somehow you don't really want to because you're scared."

"What are we going to do with ourselves now?" Pearl asked in an exhausted voice. "That's a frightening question." She listened for the siren above the noise of the parade and then she saw Frank turn and walk back inside the jail. "I really don't care," she said, "if I sit here for the rest of my life and never get up."

"Mother," Teddy said. "You exasperate me. I don't know how much more of this I can take. You always act like you're defeated, and at the same time you encourage everybody else to get up and get going."

"What are you talking about?"

"You know." He pointed to the twirlers. "You have really helped those stupid girls. It's too bad you can't do the same thing for yourself."

"That's not the sort of thing I want to hear from my son." Pearl sprang to her feet. There was a determined tone in her voice that Teddy had not heard in a long time. It almost frightened him to hear it. "These twirlers can get along quite well without us," she said. Taking her son by the arm she pulled him away from the bench and back to the street. The parade was coming through town, and the first marching band was upon them.

"Somehow, we've got to cross this street," she said, "even if we have to stop the parade to do it."

After the band had passed they dashed across the street and forced a path through a small crowd that had gathered in front of a drug store.

"Wait for me at the counter," Pearl said as they went inside. "Order something."

Teddy sat at the counter while Pearl found a telephone booth. She dialed Information. Teddy watched her writing down a number. Then she dialed again, but this time her fingers were shaking.

The phone rang several times. "Mother would call me a tramp for this," she said.

A man finally answered.

"Charles," she said. "Where did you get a voice like that, and do you have a mind to go along with it?"

"Who is this?" he laughed. "Can I guess?"

"I'm sure you can," said Pearl. Teddy had come to her side. "I have a favor to ask."

"Anything," he said.

"My son would like to ride your horses."

"When?"

"Today," Pearl answered without the slightest hesitation. "As soon as possible."

Teddy grinned.

While Charles gave directions to his house, Pearl wrote them down on the back of a paper she had been carrying in the pocket of her blazer. It was the program for the piano recital. "That was only last night," she said on hanging up the phone, "but it seems so long ago." She folded the program and returned it to her pocket. Then she removed Big Teddy's dog tags from her ankle and put them into her son's hand. "It's terrible," she said, "what it sometimes takes to make you open your eyes."

"Are you afraid?" he asked as they walked to the door.

"Only of the newness," she answered. "And that, like so many other things, will gradually go away."

On the street again, Pearl felt she was reentering a world she only vaguely remembered. For the first time in many years, she felt surrounded by all the time she needed to do everything she had ever wanted to do. As the parade passed before them, her eyes wandered to the other side of the street to the corner of the lawn where the twirlers were still practicing. Again they completed their routine without a mistake. Relieved to know that their gold metals might at last be obtainable, they shouted for joy and threw their batons high into the air. Up, up, up they went like three silver wheels spinning above the trees and into the open sky. For a moment they seemed to disappear against the white clouds. And then, they started to fall.

THIRTY

The elderly McAlister sisters, Pearl in khaki pants and a Hawaiian shirt and Wanda Gay in an organdy dress with butterfly sleeves, sat on the wedding porch of their family house and argued over the rose bushes that Pearl had planted during the night while her sister slept. She had planted a bush on either side of the sidewalk and one just outside her bedroom window. "Why was I not consulted on this very important issue?" Wanda Gay could be heard up and down the street, in backyards, living rooms and on screened-in porches. "Why do you feel as though you must slip around to get your way, Sister? Why can't we just talk about these things sensibly like everybody else? Why can't we be like other people? Once again you have taken things into your own hands and now you're forcing me to do the same. But unlike you, I issue fair warning and here it is: just as soon as the diabetic sores on my feet heal and I'm able to use the shovel again I intend to dig up those damn rose bushes and move them away from the sidewalk. You are determined to rip my fine dresses on rose thorns. You are determined to cause me distress. You are determined to be the cause of my declining health. That proves you don't love me anymore and never have."

"I didn't request a diatribe, Sister." Pearl spoke with little emotion in her voice. She was busy rolling cigarettes for the entire evening.

163

"Sister," asked Wanda Gay, "are you listening to me?"

"Not really," said Pearl. She lit her first cigarette and smoked it while rolling another. They were all the same: very thin, with tobacco tightly packed and evenly distributed from one end to the other.

"You have caused me much anguish over this planting situation." Wanda Gay was sorting through a can of mixed nuts.

"I am deeply sorry." Pearl pretended concern.

It was early May. The fireflies were swarming low over the yard which was again covered with grass, green hedges, and flowers. The supper dishes had been washed, and the cats fed. On a stool next to the swing, tea was steeping in a china pot.

Many years had passed since the McAlister sisters had made the trip to Arkansas, many years since Miss Fane's funeral and since Teddy, now a father and a practicing analyst, had traveled to Brazil to claim Frank's body and bring it home. Morehope had become a bigger, noiser town, and this did not set well with Wanda Gay. She hated noise, especially from the tennis courts.

"Why do these young people have to scream when they make a point?" she would ask. "Why can't they play with their mouths shut."

Wanda Gay was terrified of walking into the yard for fear she would be hit by another stray ball. She had already suffered a black eye and a bruise on her hip caused by tennis balls ricocheting off the roof and into her path.

"I don't want to live anymore, Sister," Wanda sighed, sweetening her tea with a cherry cough drop. A stray ball landed on the lawn near the newly planted rose bushes and Wanda Gay flinched. "I feel trapped in our very own home, Pearl. I don't feel safe walking into the yard anymore. If another ball were to hit me in the eye I think it would kill me."

"No it wouldn't, Sister," said Pearl. "The attention you would get at the hospital would keep you alive."

For a while Pearl entertained herself by blowing tiny smoke rings into the yellow light and Wanda Gay, enjoying the hint of sweetness in her tea, sat there with a smile on her face, her eyes fixed upon the lawn. Suddenly another tennis ball landed on the grass. "I am so sick of these balls flying through the air without warning," Wanda Gay said, hobbling into the yard with her teacup, which she held in front of her like an instrument of navigation. She picked up the ball and managed to bounce it across the street where a Piggly Wiggly supermarket had been built. "Why didn't they build the tennis courts behind Mr. Piggly Wiggly's food store?" she said, limping back to the porch.

"Don't spill your tea, Sister," Pearl said. "That would make you cross."

"I'm already cross," replied Wanda Gay, slowly negotiating the steps on swollen legs. "And do you know what it is this time?"

Pearl sipped her tea. Holding her cup and cigarette in the same hand, she waited for her sister's answer.

"I am still cross because you abandoned me in Arkansas with mother's cold body and ran off to rendezvous with a man you hardly knew." Wanda Gay sat back down in the swing and pushed off with her good leg. "I am also cross because you did not attend mother's funeral. Nor did you lift one finger to make an arrangement. And when it came time to bury Frank you wore loud colors to the service."

"I wore a shirt like the one I'm wearing right now, if I'm not mistaken," said Pearl. "I may have worn this very same pair of slacks, too. I, unlike you, never throw anything away."

"Disgraceful to dress in garish colors for your brother's funeral," Wanda Gay said. She was polishing her mother's cameo ring on the hem of her skirt. "You had everybody in Morehope talking about us again. The pants I can somehow accept, Sister, but the Hawaiian shirt was not appropriate."

"Frank would have liked it," Pearl said. "That's all that counts. But I know what you mean about hating the shirt. It's Charles's favorite, but I don't like him in it. I do, however, like me in it. I'm so sorry, Wanda Gay, you don't seem to share my opinion."

Pearl offered her sister some insect repellent but Wanda Gay said she didn't need it. "This diabetes is getting me down," she said. "My legs are so numb I can't tell if the mosquitoes are biting me or not."

Wanda Gay's legs were spotted with mosquitoes. Pearl sprayed them away. The fireflies also vanished, disappearing from the porch and yard and moments later turning up again in the parking lot of the Piggly Wiggly. Before long, however, the mosquitoes returned, this time attacking Wanda's neck and ears, but she felt nothing. She hurled a handful of Brazil nuts into the yard and cursed: "Goddamn Brazil and all of South America for killing Frank."

"You didn't even like Frank," said Pearl. "Why do you pretend you do?"

"I liked Brother more than you think," said Wanda Gay. "I've given up Brazil nuts, haven't I? I liked Brother, but Brother did not like me. Let's put it that way. Now don't ask me another question."

"Then you ask me something," said Pearl.

There were many questions Wanda Gay had wanted to ask her sister. She had been saving them up for a day when Pearl seemed receptive.

"Remember, Sister, you asked for it," Wanda said. "For a long time now I've wanted to ask you why you are the way you are, Pearl. I just don't understand why you do what you do, why you say the things you say, and why you dress the way you do when you know that nobody likes it. Most of all I have never understood why you married Charles on the spur of the moment, without giving it a second's thought, when you professed, and still profess, to love Big Teddy more than anybody else in the world; it just doesn't make sense to me. Charles is nothing like Big Teddy was. Charles is the opposite of Big Teddy."

Pearl sat there wondering what she would say. There were many answers sifting through her mind, and she had no idea which answer was the right one, or which was the most important one. She sprayed her sister's arms and neck and the mosquitoes again disappeared for a while. She extinguished her cigarette into a pot of sand and lit another one. "I hate tea," she said taking the final sip before setting the cup down.

"It's not any of your business why I married Charles," she began, "but since you want to know so badly I might as well tell you. I married Charles because I wasn't really in love with him. But I did like him, and I still do. I did respect him, and I still do. I realized early on that Charles would never be in my heart the same way Teddy was and still is. And that's part of the reason why I married him. I wanted to preserve Big Teddy's image. I wanted to go on living with him in spite of the fact that he had some character flaws. None of us is perfect, Sister. Are you aware of that?"

"What were Big Teddy's flaws, Pearl? You've never talked about that."

"His eyes roamed around," said Pearl. "He thought I didn't know that, but I could see. He was always looking at other women, and had he lived he probably would not have been faithful. But who's to say. He didn't live, but while he did, he was faithful. Still, I was always aware that he was looking at other women and that kept me alert. That kept my blood racing when we were together. I was always noticing who he was noticing and would go out of my way to make myself twice as appealing as the other woman. Charles, on the other hand, would not dream of being unfaithful, and that has made our marriage a little too secure for my liking. He would not dream of having an argument, only a sensible discussion, and that has made our life together a little too calm. The only time we almost argued was a few weeks before our wedding.

I refused to allow Charles to buy me a new wedding ring because I wanted to wear the one Big Teddy had given me. Only a few minutes before the Justice of the Peace married us I slipped Big Teddy's ring off my finger and gave it to Charles and during the ceremony he reluctantly slipped it back on my finger. Yes he was angry. And can you blame him? He later told me he'd felt as though he was marrying two people. I told him that he *had* married two people because I would always go on living with Big Teddy in my mind."

"Pearl," gasped Wanda Gay, "how can you live with a dead person? When Sunday died, I let him die. I buried him with that handkerchief tied around his head, and I gave him up. Why can't you be like me?"

"Oh God, Wanda Gay," Pearl said. "Where do you get all these questions? Sometimes I feel as though I am living for one reason only: to put you in the ground." She blew smoke into the yellow light and watched it drift into the yard. "As for Sunday," she said, "I'm convinced you were ready to be rid of him. He dragged you down. The fact that you don't miss him proves it. You see, Sister, if you really love someone, they are always with you no matter where they're buried, how they're buried, or how long they're buried. You don't understand this because you never loved Sunday. It was probably a relief to you when he choked to death. You probably felt like laughing."

"I did not, Pearl," Wanda Gay screeched. "I most certainly did not laugh when Sunday died. How dare you insinuate such a thing." From somewhere within the neckline of her organdy dress she brought forth a lemon drop and slipped it into her tea. "I have to admit," she confessed in a serious whisper, "I didn't enjoy seeing Sunday desecrate Mother's house by his presence in it. The day after Mother was buried, Sunday called a moving van, and by mid-afternoon we had moved in. I thought that was too fast, and so did this entire town, but that's what happened. If you had been here, Pearl, it would not have happened that fast. If you had been here, it probably would not have happened at all. If you had been here, Mother's funeral would not have been as hard on me as it was, but no, you were off somewhere getting married to a man you didn't love and knew you didn't love."

"That is not entirely true," said Pearl. "I wish to God another tennis ball would hit you in the head right now. It would save me the trouble."

"Don't get violent with me Sister, I happen to be an invalid. You do know the meaning of the word *invalid* don't you?"

"I believe so," Pearl spoke with feigned uncertainty.

Wanda Gay stood up and limped across the porch. With her back to Pearl, she listened to the squeaking swing and wondered where all the fireflies had gone. "I tried to hold my tongue, Sister," Wanda Gay confessed. "But I just couldn't. Every time Sunday sat in one of Mother's chairs, he broke it. Every time Sunday picked up one of Mother's fine old plates he would drop it. Every time Sunday sat down in Mother's porcelain bathtub, he'd get stuck and it would take me and two of the grocery sackers from the supermarket to pull him out of there. Do you know how embarrassing that was, Pearl? Do you know what anguish and humiliation and disgust I felt all over my body? The day he ripped the faucets off the wall trying to pull himself out of the tub was the day I almost lost my mind, and you were nowhere to be found. You and that second husband of yours were parading off to some horse show and couldn't be bothered with what torment your only sister was being forced to endure. So finally, after Sunday almost completely demolished the bathroom fixtures, I said, 'Sunday, I hope to God Almighty I live to see you in your grave because you're not doing me a bit of good alive.' That's when he moved down to the Texaco station where he could bathe in the car-wash facility and sleep on a pile of innertubes in the backroom. Every time I'd drive in for a refill, I'd say 'Sunday, don't come back. This is where you belong.' "

"Wanda Gay, that was the healthiest thing you ever

said to anybody and probably the most honest words you will ever utter."

"Oh no, Pearl," exclaimed Wanda Gay. Standing on the edge of the porch, she twisted the cameo ring around her finger and stared at the tennis balls littering the side yard. "I'm just like Mother, I have lived to see my faults staring me in the face. What I'm going to tell you I've never told another living soul: one Thanksgiving after Sunday left home I sent Demeris down to the Texaco station with a new handkerchief and turkey sandwich. And that was the sandwich he choked to death on. I have blamed myself for Sunday's death, Pearl. I can't help it. Do you think it was my fault? Tell me it wasn't even if you think it was, even a lie will make me feel better at a time like this."

"The sandwich was too dry," said Pearl. "That's why Sunday choked on it. You have never learned to cook a moist turkey, and you never will."

"Pearl!" Wanda turned around to face her sister. "All you have ever concentrated on is how to hurt my feelings more than you already have. You have never said what I need to hear when I needed to hear it. Why is that?"

"You laughed when Sunday choked to death," Pearl said. "I know you did. They had to give you a sedative to calm you down. That's what I heard. Your own daughter told me so."

"I hate Demeris for telling everything she knows," said Wanda Gay. "She's too much like Sunday. She even looks like Sunday."

"You laughed, Sister. Admit it and you'll feel better."

"Oh, all right," Wanda Gay said, eyeing her sister with contempt. "I did laugh when Sunday died, and if I had to do it over I'd laugh again twice as hard." A tennis ball bounced off the roof and fell to the grass but Wanda failed to notice it. "Not only did I laugh," she said. "It was worse than that. I felt a sense of relief. I felt as though I was receiving a second chance. I felt as though the entire world was at my feet, and that I had been

170

given the opportunity to do everything I'd always wanted to do."

"And what had you always wanted to do, that you had not already done, may I ask?" Pearl was flipping through a copy of the local paper.

"I'd always wanted to write a little book filled with all of Mother's sayings." Wanda Gay hobbled into the house and Pearl read the obituaries by the porch light. "So the first thing I did," Wanda Gay said from the living room, "was take out all my old notebooks and read them again. And then I rearranged all the sayings and made two handwritten copies. One of them is right here in my hand and the other one is in the library."

"I never knew you did that," Pearl said with sudden interest. She flung the paper to the floor and sat upright. "Has that book ever been checked out? I'm curious to know who would read such a thing."

"People like me," Wanda Gay replied. She reappeared on the porch, a walking cane in one hand, a leatherbound notebook in the other. With the cane crooked around an arm, she opened the book at random and began reading in a serious voice:

"'Be thorough. Be thorough, but don't overdo it, else you won't have anything to do tomorrow.' Mother said that Pearl. Isn't it good?"

"Just wonderful," said Pearl. "Makes me want to smoke this entire pouch of tobacco all at once."

"This little book is very useful," said Wanda Gay. "I have tried to pass along to Demeris everything that Mother passed along to me."

"Why on earth would you do that?" Pearl wanted to know.

"Because I, unlike you and Frank, have a higher sense of values," Wanda said, leaning forward on her cane.

"Oh, my dear, dear sister," Pearl replied. "Do you realize that Frank and I often felt responsible for you. If only we had been able to accept you as one of our own

171

flesh and blood, you would not have turned out to be the disagreeable human being you are today."

"You and Frank treated me as though I came from another planet or, what's worse, another family." Wanda Gay lifted the notebook to throw it at her sister but stopped herself before she did. "You often communicated your feelings through somebody else. 'Mother,' Frank used to say, 'Pearl and I would like for you to tell Wanda Gay to stop trying to include herself in our money-making business. We don't want her out there washing cars and changing oil with us. She's too hateful. If she wants to make money, let her think of her own way.' And then Mother would say, 'But she's your sister. Be sweet to her.' And then you, Pearl, you would say, 'No she is not our sister. Frank and I don't have a sister.' Both of you treated me as if I were totally unacceptable. And for that reason it shocks me to realize that I was grief-stricken over Frank's death and for no reason at all." She inched her way across the porch and with one swing of her walking cane she knocked the can of mixed nuts off the tea table and into the yard. "Here I have refused to eat Brazil nuts for all these years and Brazil nuts are my favorites."

"You were grief-stricken over Frank only because his death reminded you that you were no longer young," Pearl said. "And yes, you are right, we did treat you as though you were totally unacceptable. You had no personality of your own and still don't. You insisted on taking after Mother. In fact, the two of you could almost pass for twins, and that nearly drove Daddy crazy. He could deal with one of you at a time but not two of you. Do you remember the last Thanksgiving Daddy spent at home? Mother tried to get him to settle an argument that nobody, not even God himself, could settle, so he just picked up his plate and walked out. Do you remember that?"

"I have tried to forget all the unfortunate moments of my life, Pearl," Wanda said, searching her bodice for a sweet. "And I encourage you to do the same."

"There are some moments, Wanda Gay, no matter

how unfortunate, that you must never forget." Pearl spoke in a scolding voice while her sister, leaning on her walking cane, gradually lowered herself into the swing. "Let me remind you again of that Thanksgiving. At the table, Mother wanted Frank to say grace and he did, but he did not say what she told him to say. Who did, except you? Instead of using Mother's words, Frank said: 'And God, thank you for giving us our dear sweet sister Wanda Gay. But please don't tell anyone she was found floating in a ditch.'"

"I have never forgiven Frank for saying that, nor you for saying 'Amen' after he said it." Wanda Gay leaned back in the swing and pushed off with her cane. "Mother invited you to apologize and you wouldn't. She asked Daddy to take over and make you and Frank say you were sorry and Daddy just sat there and didn't say a thing. He wasn't about to take up for me. You and Frank were his favorites. He didn't think I was smart enough."

"That Thanksgiving Daddy came to the realization that he had had enough," Pearl continued. "And I felt sorry for him. He took his plate of turkey down to the body shop to eat in peace. Later on he told me that his only regret was that he didn't take all his cats with him. Mother hated those cats. And she also hated living with Daddy, but she wasn't going to admit that. She was determined to drive him away from home, I mean for good. She vowed no rest for herself until she had him and his cats out of the back room and out of the yard and out of sight."

"Pearl, I know what you're going to say," said Wanda. "And it's most certainly not true. When Daddy hobbled up to the house to take his baths he was filthy. He looked just like a tramp with grease and dirt all over him. Mother ran him off because he looked like a vagrant. She just told him to go and he went."

"No, sister, you've got it all wrong. It's going to take me an age to straighten you out, and then what good would it do. Nothing is as simplistic as you would like to believe. Daddy's exodus from this house wasn't all that easy. For a long time he came and went every day, feeding his cats in the backyard and sleeping in the little add-on room he built for himself. That went on until Mother thought of a way to run him off for good. She hired Hacienda Rodriguez to come over to the house and turn Daddy's favorite cat into tamales. Then she fed him a Mexican dinner he never forgot."

"I don't believe it!" Wanda Gay protested. "Mother loved Daddy in her own peculiar way. After he moved out for good she sent him a plate of food every Thanksgiving."

"A plate of food he wouldn't even feed to his cats," Pearl said. "After eating Hacienda's tamales he said that he would never again eat anything that came out of Mother's kitchen, and as far as I know he didn't. Mother would say, 'Take this plate of food down to Albert and tell him to try to find it in his heart to be thankful that he still has a family that remembers him, in spite of his ways.' She thought that redeemed her, you see. You, Wanda Gay, don't remember any of this because you were a total disappointment in Daddy's eyes, and therefore, you didn't have to deliver his food, but Frank and I did. 'Tell Albert,' Mother would say, handing me a covered plate, 'that we're not having cat tamales anymore. Tell him to say a prayer before he eats and maybe just maybe he won't choke to death.' "

"Don't mention choking around me again!" said Wanda, clutching her notebook to her bosom. "Just tell me what you'd tell Daddy."

"I'd deliver the message," Pearl replied. "Word for word. So would Frank."

"And what would Daddy do?"

"He would bury the food," Pearl said, "and then he would take the plate and sail it like a flying saucer over the automobile graveyard. If you were to walk out there today, you'd find enough dishes to start another family on."

"I don't believe a word of this," said Wanda Gay.

"Of course not," said Pearl. "The truth has always escaped you."

Wanda Gay, determined to ignore her sister for the rest of the evening, opened her notebook and began reading in her mother's voice:

" 'You're not finished until you're finished. Don't pretend you are when you're not.' "

" 'How dare you call attention to my own shortcomings before I've had a chance ᵗ ⁾ do so myself.' "

" 'Don't bother me with the facts. The facts aren't important. It's *my* attitude toward them that counts.' "

"I can't stand this another minute," Pearl said. She left the porch and went into the house to sit in the dark living room where the metronome was faintly ticking and the cats were walking on Wanda Gay's watercolors spread out on tables and chairs.

"The art of watercolor is my special gift." Wanda had only recently announced to Morehope.

Three months before that evening in early May, when tournament balls were falling like hail stones and the yard was flooded with light, Wanda Gay had visited Marcela Ponselle, a transient psychic, who had convinced her she was an artist. Marcela had set up her parlor in the back of a 68 Volkswagen van which she'd parked in the Piggly Wiggly lot for an afternoon. She was a black woman with a French accent, copper-colored hair, and splits between her front teeth. "I see undiscovered talents," she said gazing into Wanda Gay's palm.

For this Wanda Gay paid fifteen dollars and five more for a set of watercolors and eight sticks of a special incense guaranteed to stimulate her creativity. Within a month she had convinced the town librarian to display her paintings of flowers in one of the reading rooms.

"This used to be our family house," Wanda Gay said at the party celebrating her artistic success. "But our grandfather, Judge Fane, gave it to the town to house the library. It was right over here that Perdita Fane, our grandmother, fell down the stairs and killed herself. See on the floor there's a stain where she hit her head."

Each day she had visited the exhibition and had told everyone that she was the only watercolorist the McAlister family had ever produced and that she owed her success to the psychic ability of Marcela Ponselle.

"Oh, I would be ashamed to admit such a thing," Pearl had said. "Wanda Gay, people like you so much better when you don't express your opinions."

While Wanda Gay sat on the porch contemplating her next picture and rereading the collection of her mother's sayings, Pearl, disregarding the ticking metronome and the cats reclining on the watercolors, started a letter to her grandson, who was finishing his freshman year in college.

"I am writing to you because I need someone sensible to talk to this evening. Your great aunt Wanda Gay, as you surely must realize by now, cannot be relied upon to deliver a sagacious thought. (Is this word in your vocabulary? It is certainly in your father's.) Most recently, due to the advice of an itinerant psychic, Wanda Gay has taken up the very fine art of watercolor, and she alone is most impressed with her newly discovered *talent*. (Why do I think you already know this?) The downstairs rooms are tonight filled with her latest creations which I am supposed to say are just splendid, and at some point before bedtime I will manage to cast a few words of praise in Wanda Gay's direction, but with my eyes closed. Since discovering that she is an inspired artist, I am not allowed to enter her downstairs rooms unannounced as I might disturb the delicate balance of her creative mind. My dear Persians, all of whom have pedigrees, are also relegated to living in the upstairs rooms, as Wanda Gay leaves her paintings (sometimes she completes a dozen in an afternoon!) to dry on top of the tables and chairs and the cats have often been accused of sleeping, walking, and eating on Wanda's fine art work. Tonight the cats are downstairs again. They seem to be in awe of Wanda Gay's artistic progress almost as much as I am and have each chosen a different picture to honor with their presence. As yet Wanda Gay is unaware of their devotion. Presently, however, she will realize that the cats are sleeping on her masterpieces and this knowledge will afford her the pleasure of venting her fitful disposition upon me, her dearest sister. She will be in here telling me that she's going to have all my cats turned into tamales. Her constant threat is not, I must tell you, an original thought on Wanda Gay's part. I, like you, don't think for a minute that Wanda would render my dear cats into tasty morsels, but I'm forced to take her seriously anyway. After all, such things have been known to happen around here.

"Before I close this rambling epistle, let me thank you for coming to visit us last week. Your presence in this old house made both of us feel years younger, but there is something I must ask of you. Under no circumstances are you to tell your father that I coached you on the fine art of rolling cigarettes. This is something I learned from my father, your great-grandfather, and you are in no way to demonstrate this ability in front of your father, who has suddenly decided that smoking is bad for your health. I am alive to tell you that it is not bad for your health. At the same time I don't think you should smoke as much as I do, but if you do, it is much cheaper to roll your own. Now you know how."

"Sister!" said Wanda Gay, attempting to throw her voice through the open window.

"I'm writing a letter," said Pearl.

"Sister, I want to ask you something else if you don't mind," Wanda continued. "I'm reading here where Mother said that a dying person sees his entire life flashing before him at the moment of death. How do you think Mother knew that, Pearl? I've always wanted to ask."

"It's an old adage, Wanda Gay." Pearl's voice floated through the living room and out the screen door. "It doesn't mean anything at all." She stopped writing for a moment and contemplated the question. "Actually," she said, "on second thought, that's one of the most thoughtful questions you've ever asked."

"Do you think Mother saw her life flashing before her when she fell off the porch that time?"

"It is not always your *own* life that you see flashing before you," Pearl said as she addressed an envelope. "Sometimes it's someone else's life that you see flashing before you so quickly you cannot put words to everything you see or feel. When facing a life-or-death crisis, time seems to slow down, but the knowledge that comes to you during those moments comes so rapidly it might take a whole lifetime to assimilate. I know this for a fact because when Frank and I were in that car wreck, I knew that *he* would live through it, but I didn't know that *I* would live through it. I saw his entire life flash before me, or I thought I did. I knew that he was not going to die in that wreck, and he knew that I was not going to die in that wreck, and that's probably the only thing that kept both of us from giving up and dying of sheer fright. That car turned over at least a dozen times and we came away without a scratch, but came away knowing something about each other that we were never able to fully express. After that I was always the first to know when Frank was in trouble. I could just sense it. All my *Frank feelings* have had something to do with what I saw flashing before me when the car was turning over. I'm certain I saw his entire life from beginning to end, but the only thing I could put into words was the fact that he would not die in Morehope. He would die someplace far away, and he did."

"And what did he know about you?"

"I didn't ask him," Pearl said, sealing the envelope. "I didn't ask him because I, unlike you Sister, don't want my future told to me. He did, however, tell me what he thought I needed to know. He knew something about Big Teddy long before we knew there was going to be a Big Teddy in my life. He knew that Teddy would die early, and that I would have to bury all of you."

Wanda Gay bounced to her aching feet and hobbled

to the screen door. "I thought I would have to be the one to bury you, Pearl." She spoke with surprise. "I've always thought that, and here you are telling me I'm wrong."

"All I'm telling you is what Frank told me when we were in that wreck. He said, 'Don't worry, you'll have to bury us all.' I assume 'us all' would include you too, Wanda Gay."

For a long time Wanda Gay did not speak. She pressed her face close to the screen wire and watched Pearl. She was sitting in a Queen Anne chair. A floor lamp at her side cast a diffused circle of light on the parquet floor Albert had designed and laid without help. The light drew harsh shadows on one side of Pearl's face, but the other side was barely visible. "You don't look like yourself tonight, Sister," Wanda Gay said, her voice singing through the screen door. "But I can still recognize you by your pretty white hair." Pearl did not move except to place a hand to her throat. Her delicate fingers were gracefully arched. The bones seemed to penetrate their thin covering of flesh.

"It's too bad that *us all* included Big Teddy, Pearl," Wanda Gay said. "If I could change anything about our lives I'd change that. I'd bring Big Teddy back, because I know that's the only thing in the world that would make you happy."

The heat from the floor lamp was bothering Pearl's right eye, on which a cataract was beginning to grow. She pulled the tasseled cord and the living room was dark again except for shafts of yellow light spilling in through the screen door and the windows. In the dark it was easier for Pearl to say what she intended.

"What I'm going to tell you, I have never told anyone," she said, staring at the silhouette of her sister framed in yellow. "I have always believed, Wanda Gay, that I was in some way responsible for Big Teddy's death. I believe I caused it, or willed it in some almost inexplicable way. I believe I even suggested it. I have always believed in the power of suggestion, Sister. Big Teddy told me himself, the day he left, in fact, that he wasn't coming back. He said I had foretold it in my sleep. He told me that I had said to him: 'I will have to bury you.' He said that I had predicted that he would die far away from here and that he would not be coming back once he'd left."

"You were talking about Frank," Wanda Gay said.

"Maybe I was talking about both of them," said Pearl. "Maybe I was only talking about Frank. I don't know. At the time I was too overcome with the sadness of our separation to realize much of anything. 'No,' I remember saying to Teddy. 'That's not true. You will be back. I can't live without you.' And he said, 'Take care of my boy, Pearl.' And that, Sister, if you must know, is the reason why I have blamed myself for Big Teddy's death. I suggested it. And it happened. Maybe that's the real reason why I can't forget him. It's too painful to think of Big Teddy in his grave because of something I said."

"I'm very sorry, Pearl." Wanda Gay's voice was filled with emotion. "You probably don't believe me but I am."

"Don't feel sorry for me, Sister." Pearl sat upright in the Queen Anne chair. Her eyes were fixed on the metronome which was ticking with the rhythm of her own heart. "I'd rather have what I had for a little while than not at all. That's the only way I can look at it right now."

THIRTY-ONE

Long after Frank's untimely death and much talked-about funeral, but not many months after Wanda Gay had been laid to rest in the Morehope cemetery, Pearl sat on the porch of the house her father had built and wondered what would have happened if her brother had not gone to Brazil, if he had never robbed the liquor store, or if Bud Johnson had decided to press charges after all. "I guess he thought he was doing Frank a favor," Pearl said, glaring at the cars passing slowly along the street. "But I have my doubts. If he had pressed charges, then Frank could have stayed in jail a little longer, and if he had stayed in jail a little longer, he might have thought twice before leaving the country."

Braced against the deep chill with sweaters and afghans, Pearl sat on the porch and stared at the icicles hanging from the roof. Smoking cigarettes her grandson had left behind, she listened to the past creeping closer like a cold wind whistling under the house. While rocking back and forth in the two-seater swing Frank had built, she thought of their car wreck and wondered what it had done to them. The car had turned over and over. Her head began swimming at the thought of it.

An old acquaintance pulled into the driveway and reminded Pearl that it was winter, and that the temperature was below freezing. "Don't aggravate me!" she shouted. An arm appeared from under the afghans and pointed accusingly at the intruder. "You think I have no mind left, don't you?" She sprang to her feet. "You probably think I killed my sister too, don't you? You probably started that vicious rumor yourself. I hate this evil town."

When the car sped out of sight she sat down again and listened. Voices from the past came to her on a wind that spoke through the bamboo chimes hanging near the front door. Although she felt the presence of silence closing in around her, she could hear her life rattling through the dried cornstalks in the back yard. She could also hear Frank's voice, brought home on a cold breeze crying through the pages of a magazine left outside on a chair.

"You want to know why I married Marsha?" Frank asked. "You want to know why I married any of the women in my life?"

"That's a good place to start." Pearl replied, waving another intruder out of the driveway.

"Ask my mother." Frank's voice ripped through the brittle pages of the magazine and lodged in the air just above Pearl's head. "Mother will give you so many answers you won't know which one to choose. When it comes to the women I've married, Mother claims to be an expert. She has an opinion on everything, even things she doesn't know anything about."

Recalling the spring of Miss Fane's sixty-first year, which was also the year of Frank's robbery, Pearl, who had by now made her peace with winter, sat on the porch and listened to voices from her past. Occasionally she would remember something and laugh out loud. Occasionally a passerby would see her sitting there talking to herself and stop to ask if something was wrong. But often she would have drifted too far away to be bothered by stares and questions, even those addressed directly to her. In the last month of her life she frequently sat on that cold porch, where her parents had been married, and stared into space as though rereading her life from beginning to end.

There were certain periods of her life that gave her

much to think about and the spring of her mother's sixty-first year was one of them. That was a year of unexpected changes for the McAlister family, and a year that Pearl had relived many times.

During that year, Miss Fane, convinced that she had all the answers to her family's problems, was constantly harping on Wanda Gay about her husband's laziness. "I wouldn't live with a man like that." Pearl heard her mother's voice slicing the cold air. "At least your father worked for a living."

"Sister's husband worked five afternoons a week down at the Texaco station," Pearl said to the mailman who was trying to inch his way across the porch without being noticed. "Did you know him?" The mailman dropped the letters and turned to stare at the old woman wrapped up in coverlets and sweaters. "Mother used to say 'I have never seen my son-in-law pumping gas. Hosing down the driveway is his speciality because he can do it sitting down.' "

"I never met him," said the mailman, who was relatively new to Morehope.

"Well, you should have," said Pearl. "His name was Jerry, but everybody called him 'Sunday' because he enjoyed resting and was good at it. 'What are you doing, Sunday?' generally brought the same old exhausted reply: 'Oh, just resting, thanks.' "

Pearl laughed out loud, sending coverlets and mufflers falling to the floor and the mailman running to the street.

For a long time she stared at the letters he had dropped on the porch. Then Frank came to her: "Mother was suspicious of any man who didn't eat steak at least four times a week and Sunday didn't. He called himself a 'spud eater' and she thought that was shameful. 'We have never had a self-proclaimed spud eater in our family,' she would say. 'Even your father, for all his faults, could eat a big steak any time of day. Men are supposed to.' "

"Demeris Lee was the steak eater in the family, Frank." Pearl pulled an afghan up over her head. "You remember that, don't you. Mother always said, 'If you feed that girl too much beef, she'll grow hair on her arms and upper lip. She'll look just like Frank, and I pray to God that's not your intention.' "

"Frank is the youngest and therefore he was spoiled," Wanda Gay said. Pearl sat up straight when she heard her sister's voice. "Because he was the youngest and the only boy, he got away with murder, especially when it came to marriage. He married, and divorced, and remarried so many times no one in their right mind could keep track of it all."

"Let's not paint a picture uglier than what it is, Wanda Gay," Miss Fane said. Pearl looked around to see if anyone was behind her. "Frank has not had more than four wives but some of them he married more than once. Some of them he keeps coming back to like he can't get enough of them. The second one, however, was not his wife, not in the legal sense. He thinks I don't know that, but I do. A *real* mother can sense these things."

"Frank's women were Mother's favorite topic of family discussion," Pearl said, shaking a fist at a neighbor who was peering over the fence to see who she was talking to. "In the middle of another conversation, Mother would suddenly say: 'They were loud mouths. All of them. All of Frank's wives knew how to exhaust you with words, and I hated every one of them, starting with Jean. *Demanding* is the only word I can think of to describe her. She was never satisfied with anything anybody ever did for her. She always wanted more. Then there was the common-law Gloria, riddled through and through with hatred, jealousy, and deceit. How on earth did the woman live with that burden? And why did I fool myself thinking Frank would come to his senses? Next came Shirley, consumed with vanity and ruled by vulgarity, and when I met her I turned to Frank and I said, "Frank, the only nice thing about Shirley is you'll never be able to sink any lower." How did I know he would turn right around and make me eat my very own words? Marsha is what he brought home next, and she's nothing but a combination of all the others. Frank never has picked a decent woman. I guess he just can't recognize one, so I thank God he's never reproduced himself. That's my prayer of thanksgiving.'

"Then Wanda Gay would say: 'How do you know he's never reproduced himself, Mother?' and then Mother would say: 'Don't you dare plant in my mind the possibility that Frank could have dropped seed on this planet. That would be the greatest catastrophe known to man. Frank's too much like his father and will never amount to anything, but I can't help loving him in spite of it. He's my only boy, and that makes him special. I just wish to God Almighty he was more like you, Wanda Gay, and less like Pearl.' "

For a few moments Pearl rocked back and forth in silence before Miss Fane's voice emerged from the creaking swing.

"Poor Pearl hasn't been the same since she lost Big-Teddy-who-died-in-the-war. That's why it's necessary for her to need somebody, and that somebody is me. I most certainly am not a well woman, and I dispute the word of anyone who makes out like I am. The truth be known, I happen to be a sugar diabetic invalid with a severe heart murmur and a bad back. So I need all the attention I can get. Pearl knows I do."

"For taking her time to remarry and move away from home, Pearl always gave two answers," Wanda Gay said, her voice drifting through the closed windows. " 'Mother needs me too bad,' and 'My boy doesn't want me to.' "

"I never said anything of the sort," said Pearl, looking all around for her sister. "You and Mother made that up because you didn't like the way I was raising Little Teddy."

"You worried Mother to death with your foolish notions about child-raising," said Wanda Gay. "She was convinced you were going to starve that boy of yours."

"My son was a vegetable eater by choice," said Pearl. "That was what aggravated Mother more than anything else. She didn't believe that anybody should have a choice but her. 'If that boy turns out to be a common criminal, it's all your fault,' she'd preach. 'You will be forced to look back on your failure and say: Number one, I did not feed him a mentally healthy diet, and number two, I did not provide him with a father after Big-Teddy-who-died-in-the-war died in the war.' "

"I married again, didn't I?" Pearl shouted. "I gave my son a good father, didn't I? I tried to, anyway. And for your information I had many opportunities to remarry." Her voice carried across the street and could be heard in Piggly Wiggly's parking lot. There housewives and delivery boys turned to stare at the McAlister house where Pearl, propped up with pillows and covered with sweaters and mufflers and crocheted afghans was swinging in the cold.

"I had many, many, many opportunities to remarry," she said. A ribbon of smoke drifted from the lump of quilts and afghans and dissolved into the yard. "I had many admirers but none of the Morehope locals measured up to my expectations—nor to the expectations of my son. That's why I went for Charles."

"It's impossible for you to replace Big Teddy," Miss Fane said. Her voice came from the far side of the porch.

"Oh, for God's sake," shouted Pearl. "Shut up!"

"I raised you to expect only the very best or nothing at all," came her mother's voice again, this time from somewhere in the yard. "And that's where I failed you. I can see it now after it's too late. Oh, may the dear Lord take me tonight and get me out of my misery, for I have lived to see my mistakes staring me in the face. I raised you to expect only the best, and that's where I went wrong."

"I just wonder where you went wrong with Frank?" Pearl inquired. "I asked you that the day after Marsha shot him in the leg and you never did answer me."

"I can't help what Frank does. He's got a mind of his own, but I can help what you do, Pearl. And I can certainly help that boy of yours."

186

"I've got a mind of my own, too," Pearl informed a neighbor who was reminding her that it was winter and she was sitting on the porch talking to herself. "You have interrupted me while I was sitting here reliving my life. Now get out of my yard."

After the neighbor left the yard, Pearl attempted to return to her thoughts. Since Wanda Gay's death she had often sat on the front porch and drifted back in time. It was her greatest joy. But that day the past was moving in closer and closer. She could almost believe Frank was in the next room, that her mother was preaching to her pupils, and that Wanda Gay was still alive and carrying on her constant battle with tennis balls. Pearl sat smoking her grandson's cigarettes and allowing her mind to drift. Often she would sit there during the bitterest days and busy herself with letters, or a book of oriental philosophy that had recently captured her attention, or an occasional visitor interesting enough to be permitted to sit with her, but that day, the past seemed more tangible than ever and her memory more alive.

Toward mid-afternoon the Methodist minister, Reverend Henderson, fairly new to Morehope, paid her a visit. He wanted to clear up some matters of grave importance regarding the reputation of the last remaining McAlister sister.

"No, I did not permit an autopsy on my dearly beloved and recently departed sister, and for good reason," Pearl hissed at the minister, who wanted her to make a statement to relieve the town of the suspicion that she had in some way brought about Wanda Gay's death.

"Autopsy's are not required by law," Pearl said. "This stupid town wants everybody autopsied even before they're dead. Sister died in the hospital. Yes, I was the last one to speak to her. Yes, I gave her a drink of water only minutes before death, but I did not give it to her to wash poison down her throat. I did not hate my sister. It only appeared that I did. And, I might add, my sister did not hate me."

"Had you not been so adamantly against an autopsy from the very minute of death, no one would have suspected a thing," the minister said. "Actually it's Demeris who believes that an autopsy should have been made, and she has started the rumor that you are responsible for her mother's passing. A simple explanation from you would set so many minds at rest over this matter."

"I cannot abide this conversation any longer," said Pearl. "I, unlike St. Paul, have never suffered fools gladly." She drifted away into her own world of memories while Reverend Henderson sat there waiting for an explanation.

While he waited, Pearl heard the jailer, Sam Sticks, speaking to her brother.

"Maybe I'd better notify your family down in Texas," Sam said. "They ought to know about your trouble."

"Oh, no," Frank answered. "Just lock me up and let me stay here a while, don't send me home. I'd rather go to Hell."

To break the silence the minister gave an account of a recent automobile accident that had taken the lives of several church members. When he finished the tragic story, Pearl heard Frank say: "Don't call my family. I'd rather take my chances with Marsha. If you knew Mother, you'd understand what I mean." Pearl laughed out loud over Frank's answer.

"How can you laugh over such sorrow?" the minister asked.

Without explanation she walked inside the house and closed the door, leaving him alone on the porch.

She wandered through the dark, cold house while her thoughts traveled backward in time. Recalling the long car trip to Arkansas brought her Mother back into the house. "Pearl, you are driving too fast." Miss Fane's voice came knifing down the banister and into the living room. "Pearl, your foot is too heavy," Wanda Gay's voice followed Miss Fane's, and behind the two of them came Demeris: "Aunt Pearl, why don't you slow down."

"I must have some relief from this," Pearl said. "I

must do something sensible or I'll go mad, I'll lose my mind." She fed her cats and splashed some cold water on her face, hoping that would end her rambling thoughts. Then she sat down in one of the Queen Anne chairs in the living room and opened a little book on reincarnation, which she had read several times. "I am the last of the McAlisters," she said searching for her place in the book. "But I don't feel as though I'm the only one left. I don't feel as though anyone has gone anywhere really. They're all still right here."

She had never felt alone in that house of memories, where each room seemed to cry out with a voice of its own. She was comfortable there. It was her home. She felt no fear in knowing that she was facing the last days of her life. "If anything," she said, before opening her favorite book. "I am ready for another trip. This time I'll travel alone."

THIRTY-TWO

When Pearl's grandson was twenty years old, she wrote him a letter which she did not mail and he did not read until shortly after her death, when it was learned that Ted, not Demeris, had inherited the McAlister House. At the age of seventy-three Pearl followed her family to the Morehope cemetery where Miss Fane and Wanda Gay were buried side by side with one plot separating them from Albert, Frank, and finally Pearl.

She started the letter on a cold night in February when the ticking of the metronome, following her from room to room, changed speeds so many times it exhausted her to keep up with it. Except for her eight cats and the rooms filled with memories she was alone with the erratic ticking. Now and again she wondered if the cats could hear it too, and assumed, because of their ability to fall asleep anywhere anytime, that they could not. Sitting in front of an upstairs window that overlooked the back yard, where dried cornstalks were rattling in the cold wind, Pearl started the letter to Teddy, her son's only child. Writing to block out the sound of the metronome that haunted her solitude, she composed her letter on a yellow pad which was discovered after her funeral. She began with a firm hand, her pen cutting through the paper on every line, but she ended the letter with a delicate penmanship almost too faint to be read.

My dear and only grandson,

I am writing to you tonight, Wednesday, February 13, for so many reasons I pray that there will be time enough to get around to them all. First of all I want to ask you about that tobacco you smoke. Where can I get some of it? Nothing vaguely similar can be purchased in Morehope, but that should come as no surprise nowadays, when there are so many different brands floating about. How can any store be expected to stock them all? If you could just give me the name (brand name please) I will ask the Piggly Wiggly to order me a supply, as it is the best. I discovered this only recently when I found three of your cigarettes in the pocket of the bathrobe you left behind during semester break. Before I smoked the first one, I examined them all three carefully and they were, I am proud to say, perfectly rolled. (We are so much alike you and I. Our fingers operate the same way and so do our minds.) The reason why I wish to change tobacco is rather strange, and I'm not too sure I know what to make of it. After I smoked your cigarettes I did not hear that infernal metronome for maybe half a day. I was surrounded by a silence I could almost reach right out and touch so I spent the entire afternoon sitting on the swing and breathing the air which was extremely fragrant that day. Something had to be blooming somewhere, but it certainly wasn't in my yard, as we are in the dead of winter here in Morehope. Still, there was a wonderful fragrance. I was annoyed, however, when so many of my neighbors pulled into the driveway to remind me that I should not be sitting in the cold. What do they know. I have nothing to say to these people anymore.

Tonight I would kill for one of those cigarettes. The ticking, ticking, ticking is about to drive me over the brink, and I would do anything to scrape together the money for some of your tobacco just to see if it would put me into that state of total and silent peace once again. The doctors, of course, are useless. Not one so-called physician has been able to discover the source of this cadence I hear.

There has been a small passage of time between the last paragraph and this one. (I am wondering: Is this obvious to you?) It occurred to me only five minutes ago that you left a backpack in your room and that I had not examined its contents. When I did so between the last paragraph and the one in progress and I was fortunate enough to find half of a cigarette. Half! I have never smoked half a cigarette in my life until tonight, and I want you to know that already I feel that wonderful silence creeping in around me. I want to get down on my knees and say "Thank you Jesus," but I have not prostrated myself for many years and do not intend to perform a humiliating act during this late hour in my life. Besides, Jesus has had nothing to do with this. I am convinced, however, that I have hit upon a cure quite by accident. Your father would not agree.

Speaking of your father, this brings me to another reason for writing to you this evening. He has written to me recently of your activities there at the university, and he is not pleased with your goings-on. Need I tell you this? He tells me you have become a speed demon in that little red car of yours. (I forget what you call it.) He used the term "speed demon" several times, which I must say offended me highly. I thought it out of character for him as well as for you. I personally think the word "demon" is not correctly applied here and would prefer a substitute and told your father this via long distance telephone and he threatened to hang up on me, something he has never done in the entire time I've known him. He told me that you are a reckless driver and points the blame toward me as I am the only member of the family who has had a driver's license revoked. As I am sure he has told you, I was picked up for speeding through a red light, something I have done in this town since I've been old enough to drive. My license was not only revoked, my car keys were taken from me by force. Your father is responsible for this. He refuses to return my keys for fear I will kill myself or someone else. This is nonsense. One day soon I will remember the procedure for starting an automobile without the keys. (My father taught me to do this, but I cannot recall the steps at present writing.) I am a fast driver but a safe driver and my record is good. I have only been involved in one accident in my entire life and I was not behind the wheel. Frank was driving. Now he <u>was</u> a speed demon and I am beginning to fear that you have a great deal of Frank inside you somewhere and that is why I am writing, to give you this piece of advice: Slow down before you kill yourself.

It is not the speed that concerns me but the fact that the highways of today are too crowded with unsafe drivers, drivers who should have their licenses revoked and haven't. (Can you tell me why I have and they have not?) This is my advice to you: Find a vacant lot somewhere and drive around and around in circles.

Yes, people will think you're a lunatic, but who cares, this will not kill you, this will do you some good. If you drive in circles you will relax your mind and learn something about yourself at the same time. My father did this and I sense you are taking after him as well. It does not matter that you never knew your great-grandfather, you can still be like him in every way possible. You can also go to mind doctors such as your father who will analyze your every word, your every move and motive and facial expression, but until you look into your own family history you will know nothing, absolutely nothing, about yourself. Listen to me. I know what I am saying—You must drive carefully. You must not speed except on some vacant lot somewhere.

Next topic! Your father tells me you are going to drop out of college and take a course in diesel mechanics given in some little technological school somewhere in the valley. Do you know where you got this notion? Do you have the faintest idea that it came out of your bloodline and has nothing to do with what your father calls environmental conditioning? As you know, your great-grandfather was a mechanic and the best there ever was, but he was also a skilled carpenter and architect as well as a libertine. I would much rather see you pursue your architectural studies than spend your life in a cold drafty mechanics shop where no doubt you will take up with a menagerie of animals and paramours to keep you company. In my day you could do this and get away with it, but today the world is different. So if you follow in the footsteps of your great-grandfather, you must be willing to pay the price. Today the world does not accept the individual. It only pretends to accept the individual. I am reminded of this every time I step across the street to the Piggly Wiggly and see how people point and whisper when I pass. (And yet they all ask for my opinion on every current topic of the day. As you know I am not informed on the current topics of today because I no longer play the radio and cannot abide the television so I haven't the faintest idea what is going on in the world and for that reason I find it impossible to answer the questions put to me in the Piggly Wiggly.)

Oh, these people in this town (especially the new-comers) are impossible to get on with. They cannot understand why an old woman would want to wear nothing but pants and Hawaiian shirts. The answer is simple: I am comfortable in pants and I enjoy the Hawaiian colors.

But I also like my Ginger Rogers dress, which Wanda found just prior to her death. She claims that Mother hid it away in the attic for fear I'd put it on and never take it off. After all these years I was so pleased to see my old dancing dress once again. Naturally I put it on. Naturally it still fits me like a glove. Yes, it is old and yellowish, and yes, I looked a bit freakish wearing it, but it is still a magical dress and I have it hanging up where I can see it all the time. (Please bury me in it even if you have to fight your father over this issue. Let me reiterate. I want to make myself absolutely clear: I wish to be buried in my Ginger Rogers dress. I want a picture of Big Teddy in the coffin with me but nowhere in sight, as Charles might come to the funeral and I don't want to hurt his feelings.) I know you are curious about Charles. Everybody is curious about Charles, especially this, my first winter away from him in years. (Some people have even asked me if he died. Can you imagine the rudeness of such a remark?) Of course he is not dead. Of course he is still living. And of course I go on thinking about him every day. You must understand this: Charles and I were not deeply in love, but Big Teddy and I were deeply in love and we continue to be deeply in love and this should come as no surprise to you. I am wondering, however, just how much you know of love. Your father and I briefly touched on this subject just the other day when I made him so angry about something. (I forget what.) Anyway, before he threatened to hang up in my ear he took the opportunity to enlighten me on your recent amorous activities. I must say I was alarmed and shocked and much distressed to hear that you have impregnated three foolish girls this semester and abortions have been performed at great expense to your father. I cannot for the life of me hit upon your reasoning here so you must inform me how you are thinking these days if indeed you are thinking—it occurs to me that you might not be.

My question is this: Why do you have to engage in intercourse with these young things? It is my opinion that you should just take them waltzing, but of course you don't know how to waltz. No one your age waltzes any more. Therefore on your next trip to visit me I intend to teach you the very simple waltz steps that I know and love as this could possibly save you some trouble and your father some money. In the meantime, I pray that you will come to your senses and stop impregnating these silly girls! Has your father not told you about safety devices available on the market these days? You can buy them over the counter and this is a blessing. If you send me some of your tobacco (which has certainly done the trick tonight), I will mail at once the birth control products I purchased just this afternoon at the drugstore. I made this purchase because it occurred to me that you must be too embarrassed to ask for contraceptive products or perhaps you don't know what to ask for by name. Of course, it is your father's responsibility to provide sexual education, but since he is too busy breeding Shetland ponies in his spare time he has fallen short of fatherhood so I will take over until he regains his parental balance once again. I told the pharmacist (I forget the man's name) that I wanted two of every type of birth control device on the market. Reluctantly he displayed my request on countertop and after I examined each product and read carefully the labels I said, "Surely this isn't all you have?" And he said, "No, this is not all we have, but it is all you will ever need."

(Of course I understood right away what he was trying to do. He was attempting to humiliate me, but you see he did not humiliate me, he insulted me. There is a big difference between being humiliated and being insulted, but this is a topic for another letter.)

I felt it best to purchase only the contraceptive devices this rude pharmacist was willing to display in public. Therefore, what I will be sending you is NOT the full line of safety products but enough to get you started on the right foot. Surely in a university town you are permitted to purchase these inventions without enduring the insults I encountered in my local pharmacy.

Getting back to those impregnated girls. They are much on my mind. Aren't you ashamed? is what I want to know. But then I stop to realize who you are and who we are and the answer is too too obvious—no, of course you're not ashamed and I don't expect you to be ashamed because that side of you is too much like Frank. Did he feel shame when he took all those women and gave them God knows how many children we never found out about? No, he felt no shame because he was too busy searching and looking and trying to find. And what was he searching for and looking for and trying to find? This is my answer: Frank was looking to connect with someone capable of understanding his body, mind, and soul, and vice versa. This is what is called a karmic relationship. Do you know this term? I do because I have read five times now a little book on reincarnation, another topic which deeply interests me but does not interest your highly educated father. Let me explain reincarnation to you. It is actually very simple. In one life you may have been my mother and I may have been your evil son or your father may have been your daughter and my mother may have been your paramour. Big Teddy may have been my slave and I may have been his cruel master and Frank may have been Big Teddy's kind and loving brother. This, you see, gives us something to work on or make up for in this lifetime. Let me take it a bit further—My father may have been my lover and his father may have been my sister. Perdita may have been your wife. Wanda Gay may have been my devoted handmaiden and Fat Demeris may have been the mother of us all—isn't that a dreary thought?

(Of course karmic relationships might not exist at all. This might simply be something somebody has made up to make life more interesting and if so it works. At least for me it does.)

It is important for you to know that there are very few karmic relationships in this day and time. That is what my book says and I have found it to be true. I had such a relationship with Big Teddy, but Frank (to my knowledge) never experienced such a thing. He somehow knew that karmic relationships existed and he was always searching for one without knowing what on earth he was searching for. This is the problem so many people experience today and this is my advice: You cannot go looking. You must stay put and not go gallivanting all over the world in search of the perfect partner. Frank traveled halfway around the universe looking for the ideal woman for him and judging from the women he chose, he did everything in his power not to find what he professed to want so much. Could this be your problem too?

I can see that you have inherited some difficult genes

from our side of the family, and I do wish you could be a little bit more like Big Teddy. At the same time I wish your father could be more like Frank and throw caution to the wind and decide to live again, as he is most dissatisfied with his very conventional marriage, his very conventional patients, and his very conventional outlook on life. (I am sure Charles is responsible for this. I am also sure that your father would have turned into a complete over-mothered neurotic had I finished raising him and that is the major reason why I toughed it out with Charles.)

Still, in spite of anything I say or do or have said and have done, Teddy harbors so much dissatisfaction in life. He wants more. He begs for more. He tells me to get ready for a divorce. He threatens to walk out in search of a more harmonious union, one which will not bore him to death. And do you know what I think? I think your father will never leave your mother because he has too much of Big Teddy's faithfulness inside him. I would never say that Big Teddy was 100% faithful but he was (I believe) as faithful as a human being can be expected to be, but your father has overdone it on faithfulness, and this has caused him much discontent. He always appears to be searching, looking, and trying to find. You see, he is like Frank in that respect, only he does not have the courage to actually go out and search, look, and find. He only talks about it constantly and has almost driven me out of my right mind. Always he is longing for something else. Longing, longing, longing. Always longing for something better than what he's got. But the thing that interests me and aggravates me at the same time is that your mother is nothing like the kind of woman I expected my son (your father) to choose. The distressing thing is that Teddy has made her over to <u>look like</u> the kind of woman I expected him to choose. With hair dye, and silicon injections, and see-through blouses, and God knows what else, he has made your mother to look like the kind of woman Frank would have lost his mind over. It seems as though Teddy started out entirely in the opposite direction of Frank and somewhere in midstream (or should I say midlife) he has changed his mind and tried to back up and do things over. At this late date he has tried and tried pitifully to take Frank as his role model and to change things around, even the things that cannot or should not be changed.

It is very important (as I have said before and will say many times) to know your family history—what happened, when it happened, and most importantly—why it happened. Therefore, I am going to give you another little lesson.

Today Wanda Gay has been six months in her grave and as she is very much on my mind today I will start with her and proceed backward in time as there is no forward in time left for me. Last fall when Sister entered the hospital with a gangrenous foot, she knew her days were numbered but she refused to give up. The first thing she did was write to everyone who had ever purchased her watercolors and invite them to view her latest creations. Even in her darkest pain she managed to make a few crayola sketches of flowers which I pinned on the wall for the guests to see. Yes, the attention made her happy for a while but after the guests left she was lonely again so she sent out invitations in my name to a surprise coffee cake party. Of course, I was furious. I said, "Why Sister? Why didn't you send the invitations under your own name?" (Yes, I raised my voice in the sickroom, but it irked me sorely and reminded me that we do not act alone even when we think we do. It reminded me that we are sometimes too influenced by all that has gone on before us. And I do mean ALL.)

"Sister," she said to me, "it is not polite to give yourself a surprise party. That's why I signed your name to the invitations."

Yes, we had another public altercation that lasted quite a spell. Yes, everyone in the hospital heard us. No, I am not ashamed. Why should I be? You must remember who <u>you</u> are and who <u>I</u> am and who <u>we</u> are and then

199

you will know why I am not ashamed and neither was Wanda Gay. She commenced complaining and agitating over the same old worn-out subjects, and she kept this up until the hour of her death, when she accused me once again of being a traitor. (Perhaps you already know this?) Shortly before her last breath she gained strength and found pleasure in telling me that she could not find it in her heart to forgive me for abandoning her in Arkansas with Mother's cold body. That's exactly the way she always put it, and of course I felt like slapping her every time she broached the subject. All of my life, it seems, I have had to work to resist the temptation to wound Wanda Gay permanently. Every time we got together we fought. We couldn't even agree on which tomato was the best, so after she passed away I was not surprised to learn that many people thought that I was responsible for her death. This vicious rumor started because I refused to allow an autopsy.

Your aunt, as you surely must know, died of diabetes, an inherited disease. (Please remember to get yourself checked each year.) She would never maintain a proper diet, and it was her constant craving for sweets that killed her. You will hear it said that I contributed to her death by secretly sugaring her coffee every morning. Do not believe this. It is not true. I may have wanted to on occasions but somehow resisted the temptation. She did, however, carry an assortment of hard candies tucked away in her brassiere.

When I saw her in the hospital for the last time, she (being aware of her imminent death) wanted me to promise that I would hide Mother's cameo ring in a safe place where Demeris would never find it. I told her I would make no such promise, not even on my own sister's deathbed.

"Then what are you going to do with it?" Wanda Gay asked. "Don't let Demeris get her dirty hands on it."

"Sister," I said, "I know exactly what I'm going to do with that damn ring, but you're going to have to sit up first." Then I cranked up Wanda Gay's hospital bed and placed the ring into the very back of her mouth just as far as I could get it. Then I forced her to drink a glass of water to make sure the ring went all the way down. After that she said, "Sister, that was the nicest thing you have ever done in your life. Because of you I can die in peace." (Now you know why I refused to have an autopsy.)

Suddenly the color returned to her face and her strength was all at once renewed before my very eyes. Oh no, I thought, now that the ring is provided for, Wanda Gay isn't going to die.

She just sat there staring at me with those little mean-looking (but not really mean) eyes of hers and presently she said, "Sister, tell me one more time. Why did you do it? Why did you abandon me in Arkansas with Mother's cold body? I have never forgiven you for that."

"Wanda Gay," I said, "you seem to be gaining too much strength sitting up." I cranked her bed down as far as it would go and then I leaned over her and spoke directly into her face. "Oh yes, you have too forgiven me," I said. "You just don't want to admit it out loud. I can see into your mind and I know for fact that I have been forgiven." Then she died with the sweetest smile I'd ever seen on her face.

Now let me explain Demeris's part in all this. The moment Sister closed her eyes for the last time I discovered that Fat Demeris and her five fat daughters and I don't know how many grandchildren had been standing in the doorway for a long time without my realizing it. This is how sneaky Demeris and her lot can be. You must watch out for them. As soon as Sister was pronounced dead, Demeris started in on me by repeating her mother's dying words. She said she would never forgive me not only for speaking my mind to Wanda Gay on her deathbed but also for abandoning her in Arkansas with Mother's cold body and so on and so forth.

Then Demeris started asking me why I had given Wanda a drink of water. What was in the water? she wanted to know. Did Wanda ask for the water? Or did I force it upon her? Even in my old age, I am perceptive enough to realize that Demeris thought that I had administered a liquid poison to her dying mother. I also realize that most people would stand up and flat out deny having done such a thing, but I did not. I looked Demeris straight in the face and I said, "Poison, Demeris. Poison was in the water. Isn't that the answer that you want to hear? Isn't that the answer that will make you happy?"

Then she commenced screaming and crying and calling me a murderess right there in the hospital. Next she started searching Wanda's fingers for that ugly and unlucky ring. She searched the bedcovers and the floor and the pillowcases and finally I spoke up. "Demeris," I said. "Listen to me. You will never find that cameo because I buried it in the courthouse square just this morning." Then she commenced calling me a thief as well as a murderess so I said, "I see you are a woman of strong but erroneous opinions."

Having said that, I marched myself into the director's office where I announced that I had already signed over all my property to the county hospital but in the event of autopsy I would change my last will and testiment at once. (You know how they are here in Morehope, they will believe anything you say as long as you say it with authority and conviction and courage and that's exactly what I did and have always done.)

After making my wishes known in the office, I strolled back into Sister's room and I said to Demeris, "You will never, not even with bloodhounds or geiger counters, find the exact spot where that ring is hidden, so you may as well give up right now."

Once again she commenced screaming, "You killed my mother with poison!"

To this I replied, "Believe as you will, Demeris. There is nothing I can do or care to do about the quality or condition of your mind."

(Now you know why Demeris has every other citizen

in this town thinking I am a kleptomaniac as well as murderess. I cannot go into any of the stores anymore without the sales clerks trailing me, watching my every movement to see if I am of the mind to pocket something. Since Wanda Gay's death I have not been able to set foot inside the Piggly Wiggly food chain or stroll across my yard without facing harsh accusations and rude stares. Ask your father how I feel about people who stare. I pray you are not given to this always offensive habit.)

Getting back to Demeris. I don't care one bit if she or any of her dull-minded offspring ever forgive me for anything that I have or have not done to them or to Wanda Gay. In fact, I would prefer not to be forgiven by Demeris or anyone associated with her, but with Sister, it's different. I know in my heart that she forgave me because we both knew that there was nothing really to forgive. In spite of how it must seem to you and everybody in this town, we were and are (for the most part) a forgiving family even when we do not forget that which we forgive. And Wanda Gay (as everyone knows) did not forget any transgression committed against her or against Mother. Occasionally we would be sitting on the porch and out of the blue, often in the middle of another conversation, she would let it slip that she considered it a selfish and thoughtless act of disrespect that I ran off with Charles and did not have the common decency to show up at Mother's funeral.

Consider it what you may, that's exactly what I did and I am glad to this day that I did it. Yes, I was frightened at first. Then the newness of the relationship worn off a bit and then in spite of the fact that our children got along and still do I became bored with life on the ranch, especially in the spring and summer when Charles was never at home. That time of year he and the boys worked the horse shows and I sometimes went with them and worked as a groom. I braided so many tails and manes and washed so many hooves until I never wanted to see another horse again. Of course your father loved every minute of it, as did Charles's two sons. The three of them were here two weeks ago and all they talked about was horses, horses, and more horses. It was enough to drive a sane person completely over the edge but I endured it all without complaint.

As I was saying, I was BORED at the ranch all by myself and BORED at the horse shows too, but I managed to struggle along because (as I believe I have said) your father needed a sensible father and Charles's sons needed a sensible mother and I tried my best to fill that role in spite of the fact that I was always hearing things that other people weren't hearing. This I'm sure reduced my sensibility at times. I'm talking about that tick, tick, ticking in my right ear, only the right one. I have always thought that I was haunted by Mother's metronome, but now I'm beginning to wonder if there isn't some sort of physical deformity in my ear, a pressure on the drum caused (like so many unexplainable things in my life) by that accident Frank and I had. Please don't get me started on that accident as I will never finish this letter and I must finish this letter because I need to clarify some of the things I've said about Charles, else the image of an odious monster will fix itself permanently in your head.

I don't mean to be painting an unpleasant picture because it wasn't unpleasant at all. Charles and I had a fairly good life together when he was at home, which was about half the year, but still I was depressingly bored on the horse ranch. And who wouldn't be after living with Mother all those years. Pity you never knew her. You will hear all kinds of frightful stories about how mean she was, and yes, all that is true. Mother was mean, but there was something else about her that made it all bearable, something rather difficult to explain unless we speak your father's language and then only a handful of people in the world would understand what we were talking about, so what's the use. What was it about her? Well, you see, it's quite simple really—Mother entertained us—Even when she was angry and hateful and rude, she was entertaining to be around. This is so hard for people to understand nowadays, but it's true. She entertained us and we entertained her. When we came together, sparks flew left and right and at times, I admit, we got carried away and hurt each other. We were, at times, horribly cruel. But what else did we have to do here in Morehope? It was the same with Big Teddy, only more agreeable. Sparks flew when we were together also, but Charles and I never had anything remotely similar to this in our relationship. The most disconcerting thing about Charles was his odor. He smelled of horses. Our bed smelled of horses, our clothes smelled of horses, our automobile smelled of horses, and when I started dreaming that I had married a man who was half horse I decided it was time to make some changes. By then the boys were grown, or thought they were, and didn't really need us anymore, so we finally came not to an end but an agreement. I could not bear to traipse around like a gypsy from horse show to horse show and I could not bear to wait all spring and summer and half the fall for Charles to come home. So I decided to divide my time. That was exactly ten years and three months after Frank robbed the liquor store and my last Frank feeling turned into another reality.

Let me back up a bit because this is something you should know. Frank remained in the Canton jail for about two months and then he was thrown out. After that he did not return to Marsha, thank God, and he did not marry again either. What he did was return to his construction company for a year before he was sent to Brazil. I had a feeling that he would never return alive and I begged him not to go, but you see what good that did, don't you? He had been hired to build a highway and two bridges through the jungle and so he picked up and left. He finished the job and stayed on in Brazil where he said he was happy. Then the next thing we knew he had died of a heart attack. During the entire time he was in South America I received three little notes from him and each time he assured me he was alone and enjoying being alone. In the last one he said that he had not yet learned enough Portuguese to know what was being said about him and was beginning to feel that he was getting to know himself for the first time in his life. He never mentioned a desire to return.

Not long after receiving that last note I was sitting on the porch at the ranch when this Frank feeling swept over me. I knew immediately he had died. That was the year your father finished his Ph.D in psychology. He wrote his dissertation on the disintegration of the American family and Wanda Gay always asked me why he had chosen that subject. The answer, of course, is so simple, too simple to explain to Wanda Gay, so I never tried. By then your father was so smart, or thought he was, until none of us could talk to him without getting a headache, so we decided he should go to Brazil to claim Frank's body and bring it back to the States. While he was there he chose the most elaborate coffin money could buy. It might have been made of ebony, I don't know. It was black and shiny with lots of carvings all over it and it captured the attention of this entire county. People came from everywhere and stood on line outside the funeral parlor for hours just to get a look at Frank's casket, which was sealed with very large, odd-looking screws. Everybody had a few things to say about that casket, and a few things to say about Frank too, what they could see of him. On top of his coffin there was a small glass window covered by a lid with a handle on it. Naturally Wanda Gay was the first to open it. And of course there was no light inside so she couldn't see a thing and immediately convinced herself that the coffin was empty.

"How much sense does it take to bring home an empty coffin," she screamed at your father. Everyone turned and looked at her and it was very embarrassing. Shameful but totally expected, as Mother might have said. For what seemed like eternity Wanda Gay ranted at your father for not inspecting the contents of the coffin before bringing it home. Then someone had the presence of mind to put a flashlight in Wanda's hand. She shined the light through the little window and that's when she discovered that Frank was in there after all. His face was bloody and bruised and his shirt was ripped. Well, that gave Wanda Gay something to talk about the rest of her life. Till the day she died, in fact, she cursed Brazil for not having what she called the national decency to wash our brother's face before sealing him up for good. For the rest of her life no one could mention Brazil without her exploding into a fitful description of Frank's untidy appearance and how she and Demeris had to clean him up all by themselves. I would have stopped them had I known.

This is what happened. The night before Frank's funeral Demeris and Wanda Gay were sitting up with the body and when everyone left the funeral home they somehow managed to pry the little window off the coffin. Then Wanda took a long-handled paint brush and a bowl of alcohol and cleaned Frank up. With a long fork she managed to arrange one of Mother's linen napkins over his chest to cover up the ripped shirt and then Demeris replaced the window and screwed it down. The next day Wanda told me what they had done. Naturally I was mortified and told her not to tell anyone for fear we'd be locked away permanently but of course she paid me no mind. Not only did she tell everyone what she and Demeris had done, she insisted on leaving a flashlight sitting on top of the coffin so Frank's friends could see him one last time if they wanted to. That's when we locked horns. "Wanda Gay," I said, "that is absolutely grotesque. Only you, the carrier of all the mental illness inherited from our mother and our mother's mother, would think of such a thing."

And then Wanda Gay said, "Sister, how dare you argue with me at a time like this. I happen to be a sugar diabetic invalid with a severe heart murmur and a bad back and you are not to cause me undue stress excitement or torment at a time like this. All you and Frank ever concentrated on was how to make me feel inferior to the human race and I will not stand here over his dead body and endure further humiliation. Since Mother's death my life has not been easy and you know it. First of all Sunday took it upon himself to get so fat he couldn't get in and out of a car so he took up residence at the Texaco station and then Demeris at the age of seventeen ran off and got married to a man who had not a penny and not a job and not a shred of hope for betterment. After that I wanted to kill myself. After that I was all alone, and I don't like living alone, Sister. What I need is to feel needed by somebody who needs somebody and that somebody is you, Pearl. You probably don't realize it, but it is. Your place is with me. My place and your place are the exact same place. I don't like living in Mother's big old house all by myself."

For the first time in my life I felt sorry for Wanda Gay. She had put on some weight. Her hair was going grey, and there was such sadness around her mouth. So I said, "Well, Sister, now you don't have to live all alone, because I have come home not only to bury Frank, I've come home to stay awhile. In about two days I'll make you sorry for it too."

"No, you won't," she said. "I have so desperately needed someone. I need to feel alive again. I need a jolt. I need something to shock me."

I took her at face value. "You know, Wanda Gay," I said, "I surely do hate to tell you this, but I'm going to anyway. You drove your husband to take up residence in that old Texaco station. You fattened him up because you didn't want him to touch you ever again. And what's more you drove your daughter away from home at an early age because she was tired of sleeping on a borrowed bed. You made her feel as though she'd deprived you and Sunday of a marital relationship and nothing could be further from the truth. You are evil, Wanda Gay." (I didn't mean one word of this, you understand, it was just something to say to bring Sister's energy up.) "You've always been evil," I told her, "and you know who you got it from, don't you."

Then over Frank's coffin, she screamed at me, "Sister, I will not stand her and absorb any more ugly comments from you or anybody else. You have always said the meanest things to me and I will never forgive you either. I was not found in a ditch like you and Frank used to say. And I am not responsible for my husband's weight, choice of residence, or death. Nor am I responsible for my daughter's reproductive drives. I will never forgive your contempt as long as we both shall live under one roof."

And that's when I said, "Wanda Gay, that's exactly what I wanted you to say. Now let's go look at Frank one more time."

So for the last twenty or thirty some odd years, I don't know how long, as I can't count anymore, I divided my time between the horse ranch, which was supporting itself, and our old family house, which Wanda Gay and I had jointly inherited. During the warm months, when Charles was on the road showing his horses, I returned to Morehope and tried to keep Wanda Gay from going completely crazy. Each spring just as soon as the first green buds appeared Wanda would call me and say, "Sister it's time to come home now."

So I would return to Morehope and that would make Wanda very happy, although I was the only one who realized it. She would sit on the porch and fuss or shout instructions to me while I worked in the yard. I hauled away the gravel a bucket or two at a time and gradually replanted the garden. Eventually the yard started looking nice again. Wanda Gay took all the credit of course. She said it was her green thumb that caused the grass to take root again but it was actually mine. When the garden club asked her to join, she was overjoyed. She spent her winters worrying whether or not I would return to make things grow for her. "Sister," she would say over the telephone, "if you don't come back and work the yard I might be thrown out of the club. You don't want that, do you?"

"No," I would say, "I don't want that, Wanda Gay. I'd do anything to keep you happy."

Every spring I would return with new ideas for the yard. I would work hard until the end of the summer when the first cool breath of air would come blowing through my bedroom window and then I would return to Teddy-Charles. By then the boys were away in school or working and it was just the two of us. We would stay home by the fire all winter or occasionally we would go dancing and sometimes I would even find myself missing Wanda Gay.

What finally broke us up and drove me back to Morehope for this last year was Charles's inability to live with Big Teddy. You know I have never been able to forget him. No one has ever taken his place, not even Charles. The last year we were together he kept telling me that I talked to Big Teddy in my sleep almost every night. He said I told him to get ready, because I was going to join him again. Sometimes I don't know what would come over me but I would forget Charles was Charles. Sometimes I would call him Big Teddy and he would remind me that Big Teddy had died in the war. Then I would fly into a rage over this somehow forgotten piece of information. That began happening too frequently. It was too difficult for Charles to go on competing with Teddy, so this last summer I decided not to return. Charles is much better off without me as he is pretty old and deserves his solitude and besides I don't plan to be around much longer. I feel Big Teddy is very close to me now. I always feel that he comes close during the winter, but this winter he is particularly close.

Shortly before Wanda Gay went to the hospital at the end of last summer we were sitting on the wedding porch and she asked me if I ever thought about Big Teddy. "Mostly in the winter," I said. "Not too much in the warm months but I do feel close to him when it's cold and everything has gone to sleep."

I have come to realize that you cannot live with the dead on a full-time basis, not if you want to go on living, and at some point after Mother jumped off the stairs I decided that I wanted to go on living. Charles helped me to decide to live again, but I found out that you don't spring back to life again like a seed sprouting. It's much more gradual. After you have been pulled all the way down by death it takes a long time to recover, and if you do recover you are certainly not the same person. As far as I'm concerned I have never completely recovered from having known and lost Big Teddy. I feel as though my life has been lived on a part-time basis. Every winter I go back to Teddy or he comes back to me. In the winter he is as much alive for me as he ever was when he was actually living. That's why I know that I will die during the winter. Not too long ago I told Wanda Gay that I would die on a very cold day when the trees were black and leafless and the dried cornstalks were rattling. You should have seen her face.

"Sister," she said, as if completely out of breath, "if I thought that way I'd move someplace where it was blistering hot all the year round."

Wanda Gay failed to understand what I meant. She could not grasp the reality of her own life, let alone mine. "Even if I moved to the tropics," I told her, "there would still be winters. And even if Charles were with me I would still be married to Big-Teddy-who-died-in-the-war."

It was almost dawn when Pearl finished the letter. She heard the cornstalks rattling in the wind and the metronome ticking away on top of the piano. Leaving the yellow pad on a stack of books, she wandered from room to room. Cats slept on tables, chairs, and stools, and lace curtains hung motionless like waterfalls that had frozen during the night. The old, dusty house seemed to be holding its breath and Pearl felt as though she was holding hers right along with it. She fed her cats for the last time, washed her face, and put on her Ginger Rogers dress.

With only a shawl thrownover her shoulders, she said goodbye to her house and cats and entered the cold, grey morning. Leaving the front door standing wide open, she walked toward the business district, the hem of her dancing dress swept the sidewalks and her white hair flew wildly in the cold wind. But Pearl did not feel the cold, not even when the garbage collector reminded her that it was winter. "I know it's winter," she answered without stopping or looking around.

Through the town she strolled, as though on her way to a dance. She held a faint smile on her face, and her arms poised in front of her as if an unseen partner were guiding her steps. It was St. Valentine's Day. Store windows were decorated in hearts and red ribbons, but Pearl was not aware of the date, nor did she notice the mixture of snow and sleet that was beginning to fall.

She cut across the courthouse square to avoid walking past the police department. Then she skirted around the depot with steps measured by the ticking only she could hear. Down the railroad tracks she went, leaving pieces of her gown clinging to the spikes and ties. Across the trestle she strolled without the slightest concern for the possibility of oncoming trains or a misplaced step. On the other side of the crossing she began looking for the automobile graveyard. "It has to be right in here somewhere," she said. "Surely it still exists."

In the distance, barely visible over brush and saplings, was a pile of rusty tin and the skeleton of a steel frame. "There it is," she said, heading toward what was left of her father's shed. Searching for the deep ruts that once circled the mechanics shop, Pearl walked around and around the pile of tin until she felt as though her feet had found the correct path. Then she followed the frozen creek that bisected the graveyard and soon she was deep within the vine-covered wreckage.

"I wonder what ever happened to that Plymouth,"

she said, strolling among the cars. Trees were growing out of some of them. Others were filled with brush and weeds and beer bottles left behind by the local teenagers.

For a moment she thought of her father and wished she had spent more time with him during his last days. She wondered if he had forgiven her for marrying against his wishes. "We were a forgiving family," she reminded herself. "Even when it seemed as though we were not." For a moment she wondered what would have happened had she taken her father's advice and not married Big Teddy. "I had no choice but to marry him," she said, her breath freezing in the air. "It was meant to be."

From some place far away she heard a waltz being played by a brass band. As the music came closer, the ticking of the metronome gradually vanished and she began dancing in the snow and ice. "I have always loved a waltz," she said, turning on thin, feeble legs. Suddenly her eyes fell upon a familiar shape. "I think that might be it." She stopped dancing abruptly. She lifted her long skirt above the dried weeds and grass and walked toward a car that seemed better preserved than the others. She leaned over the roof and wiped away the frost. "I believe this car has our names on it," she said, running her fingers over the roof until she found the grooves and followed them. "Yes," she said, as if reading braille. "This is it. This must be it."

The driver's door had been removed, and the front seat was resting at an angle. The steering wheel was covered with mud and the floorboard was overgrown with brown grass and weeds. "This is it," Pearl said as she slid into the car. "This is our old Plymouth."

In the distance the snow clouds parted, allowing a single shaft of golden light to fall upon the wrecked automobile which was glistening with ice and frost. Pearl sat in the driver's seat and placed her hands on the cold steering wheel. Directly above her the clouds were dark and turbulent, but through the frosty windshield she could see nothing but the bright column of light rising through

213

the trees and refracting in the ice prisms. Colored light fell onto her lap, painted her arms and face with patches of red, yellow, and blue. "So beautiful," Pearl said. She felt the car moving upward, as though the tires were being filled with air. In the distance the brass band faded into the sound of the car being started. "This is the way it should be," she said, holding the colored light in her hands.

Sleet fell upon the car in sharp notes as though in the distance many pianos were being tuned at the same time. Ice had formed on the skirt of Pearl's only dress. Her stockings had fallen to her ankles and were frozen. Ice was on her shoes, her hair, and her shoulders. But she did not notice the cold. She welcomed it. At last it had come, her final winter. And she was glad. While snow clouds hung low over the graveyard, the rising sun burned a narrow path through a world that was barren and leafless and ready to set her free. "Teddy," she whispered with a smile, as the engine raced and the car sped away into the light.